Francesca Rendle-Short was born in 1960, the fifth of six children, and grew up in Queensland. She has worked in radio, eduction and publishing. Her poetry and short stories have been published in various literary journals and magazines. Her novella, *Big Sister*, was published in 1989 (Redress Press) and she was the winner of the 1995 ANUTECH Short Story Award.

T0159860

imago

Francesca Rendle-Short

Spinifex

Spinifex Press Pty Ltd
504 Queensberry Street
North Melbourne, Vic. 3051
Australia
spinifex@publishaust.net.au

First published by Spinifex Press, 1996

Edited by Janet Mackenzie
Typeset in AGaramond by Claire Warren
Cover design by Liz Nicholson, Design Bite
Made and printed in Australia by Australian Print Group

National Library of Australia
Cataloguing-in-Publication data:

CIP

Rendle-Short, Francesca Tyndale, 1960– .
Imago

ISBN 1-875559-36-1
A823.3

This publication is assisted by the Australia Council, the
Australian Government's arts funding and advisory body.

For Ned and Hephzibah.

Acknowledgements

MY THANKS go to the many people who have given me support and encouragement in different ways throughout the course of writing this book. To Glyn Lehmann for the music to *Sweet River* and Susan Mitchell for advice on speech patterns. My thanks to Sara Dowse for her excellent editing. Also, to Michael Traynor, Pling, Fiona Edge for the lino-cut, Elisabeth Fagan-Schmidt for the inspiration of her grandmother's *Calendar of Cakes* (SA CWA), Di Brown, Moya Costello, Janet Mackenzie and Fiona Inglis. To all at Spinifex Press, in particular, Jo Turner, Lizz Murphy and Susan Hawthorne. And especially, to Jonathan Nicholls, Hephzibah Rendle-Short and Ned McKenzie.

Author photo by Jonquil Mackey.

The illustration on page 14 is from Betka Zamoyska, *The Ten Pound Fare*, Viking, 1988, Commonwealth of Australia copyright reproduced by permission. The epigraph is from Mary Morris, *Maiden Voyages: Writings of Women Travellers*, Vintage Books, 1993. Permission granted by International Creative Management. Copyright © 1991 by Mary Morris.

To wait . . . is in a sense to be powerless . . . If we
grow weary of waiting, we can go on a journey.

Mary Morris, *Maiden Voyages*

Contents

MARJ WAS fat. But it wasn't only her bulk that interested Molly. It was the colour and texture of the skin—taut, brown, hardened. Skin stretched and hair bleached. Good-looking, hard-working skin.

Molly wanted to get into her neighbour's skin, clothe herself with it, and feel its dryness and colour with cool fingers.

PART ONE

between two acts

MOLLY ROSE Moone (for that was her name in the beginning) dreamt of worms the night before she married Jimmy
Brown in Tooting Bec. Milky sticky wet worms wriggled
and fed off one another in clumps all over the bed. Breast
deep. The young couple were on their way to Australia.

Twenty-eight years later, cradled in the silky humidity of
a Queensland summer, she dreams of worms again. Only
this time, with Jimmy's aerogram scrunched beneath her
pillow and with bags packed on the floor ready for a journey
south across the border, Molly dreams of worms, milky and
sticky, but they're still, quite still. These motionless worms
aren't dead, but caught in the pause between two acts.

The waiting, THE WAITING, she dearly wants to scream,
has been nigh on impossible, a litany of broken memory
pieces, ocean debris washed up onto warm and gleaming
sand. And then in one movement, unexpectedly, quite by
chance it seems on the surface, the time is ripe and her
waiting is over. It is that easy. She is inviting herself to a
feast. To sit at the table and to eat, in an act of communion.
And the sand, that zip of whiteness caught between the wide
body of water and solid ground, is an ally.

The beach had been empty that morning. There was a storm
overnight and the sand was damp, its skin pock-marked,
the finer grains washed away leaving the weightier pebbles
exposed. The surf was flat and the colour out deep a dull
grey. A stray tumble-weed rolled haphazardly down from

the sculptured dune, delicate and nimble, the whole stage to itself.

Somewhere on the firm sand where the slippery layer of salt water is never far from the surface, a lone figure strode the length of the beach in bare feet. She took large deliberate steps, head down, glancing up every now and again out of habit to view her possible destination, where to a seasoned eye the dune changed shape. She knew the long stretch of beach well, but this was no ordinary morning exercise. Her mind was troubled. It wasn't the walk or the surf or even the nature of the storm that possessed her. Nor was it her daughters who lay sleeping, cocooned in their cotton sheets. It was something else, a pestering irritant rooted in the past that wouldn't leave her alone, like a sore that had never healed.

She hadn't slept well. Her night had been interrupted with the shutting and opening of windows and the thrum of rain on the galvanised roof, and she'd awoken from a fitful doze to the descending chilled air just before the rising sun lightened the sky. She was thinking about her need to make a journey. And if she could just concentrate on the practical details of that journey, make a mental note to have the Chrysler's oil and water checked, pack and repack in her mind all they needed to take while wondering how everything would fit in the car, then she wouldn't have to think about what lay before her. She wouldn't be forced to look into the oozy sore beneath the slick surface of skin. But her hands were a giveaway. It was as if her body gave her no choice but to take heed. No amount of flicking her arms into the air with rhythmic precision, as if she were training for a marathon walk, would be able to hide the tense posture. Behind whitened knuckles she gripped conflicting sources of pain and pleasure. In one hand a crumpled aerogram. In the other, her salvation, a small sprig of boronia plucked from a bush growing in the front garden of her neighbour. Half awake, she'd grabbed it earlier as she came out. The fresh new growth seemed vulnerable and fragile, encouraging a spirit of comfort in Molly.

The frantic pace of her walk slowed. Her arms relaxed enough for the drum-tight fingers to loosen their grip.

She would dry Jimmy's letter when she got home, her sweat had made his ink run. She would flatten the crumpled lines with a hot iron, then retrace his smudged phrases with her own handwriting, teasing out the meaning of his words on paper before committing them one at a time to memory. On her way south they'd lodge there in the cool recesses as a reminder of what might be. This was the hope, the promise of the boronia.

swimming to safety

SHE WAS inviting herself to a feast.

There was no time to lose.

To sit at Marj's table.

She would see her again.

As she drove home these thoughts ruffled the calm she'd possessed on the beach. Excitement cavorted and fairly leapt through her body. A raw energy seized her muscles so that it was hard knowing where to put her hands and legs, and her mouth was so dry her tongue stuck to the roof. She needed a drink of cold beer to fizz across her lips and wet her tongue. With a glass in one hand she would be able to plan the journey sensibly.

Much later, with quick jolty movements, she moved about the flat from room to room reaching for things to pack, her arms waving around her body like the legs of an insect on a hot desert dune. She stuffed as much as possible into a blue snakeskin suitcase bought from Vinnies for five dollars—changes of clothes, Panadol, tampons for the girls, a new dress and matching lipstick to impress Marj with, a must, lemons from the market—she'd need to get more fruit—clean underwear and water bottles. There was a box of food for the journey, and she packed pillows and sleeping bags for the overnight vans they'd stay in.

She slammed the suitcase shut and sat on its cardboard lid to press the locks into place. In that moment Molly began to realize what she was doing. The chance (or was it driven by necessity, of what will be will be?) the chance nevertheless, to drive out of Queensland to the nation's capital had dropped into her hand like one of Marj's ripe loquats. Hadn't it? All she had to do now was eat. But she was caught in the pause between the coming and going. Would Marj want to see her? Her memory slid around on its mooring. It was how she imagined death to be, seeing everything in a flash but in slow motion, all the details of a life in an open picture book, the sorting of dross from gold.

The girls would be home from school soon. They would be wanting explanations. Her blood was warm, her cheeks pink. She looked out through the flat's sliding double doors, across the tops of the high-rise buildings at the vegetative balconies and matching pools of blue water on the rooftops. But it was the silence that ate at her. The silence of the outside view and the silence between the four walls. While in her head a noisy group of musicians started to rehearse.

Molly tried to stand, hoping to gain support from the thick coastal air. And she began to hum, her mind swirling with memories of those waiting years awash with obsession and love. At first a sweet tune, Marj's tune, the spiritual Marj would sing over and over and over again, beckoning her even now from out of the past, *Where the river oh the sweet river flows*, but then with her legs misbehaving as if fashioned out of soft clay, she teetered. She tried leaning back into the thickness, looking for support. The bass line strummed in her ear and the violins exploded in shrill tones. It became too much to bear, the weight of the past growing way out of proportion, and she lost her balance. Thrashing frantically, she tried to swim through the heat, away from the deafening cacophony to safety she knew not where.

She couldn't wait any longer!

And in that instant, she fell to the carpet with relief. The feeling was the same as waking suddenly from a nightmare to sense the sheets top and bottom, and the certain comfort of another human body. And all the errant parts of her body came ricocheting back into position as though connected at the joints by large rubber bands. Her muscles and bones were elastic in substance. She was being transformed.

Quite still, Molly listened out for the familiar turn of the key in the lock followed by Kate and Sarah's footfall across the threshold and onto the kitchen lino. Was she on the floor for ten minutes or half a day? She didn't know and it didn't matter. The important thing was to be on the road in the morning with her two girls, heading south, the waiting all but over. It wouldn't matter how she started once she got going. The relief was immense. And the wheels of the chocolate-coloured Chrysler would murmur in submission.

a yellow eye

IF SHE were to drive to the high country, to a dream of a planned city, to view its fabulous bicycle paths and green buffer zones, monuments and fountains, its botanical gardens and native suburbs, its famous coloured cement buildings and gas barbecues, she'd want to be there by the end of the week—Easter Friday. Marj would want it that way. Sometimes the timing of things can be quite accidental.

Remember Marj.

Begin by snatching a warm egg from beneath a dusty pullet. Feel the shape, the smoothness and rigidity of the tan shell. The insides burst with possibilities, especially at Easter . . . fertility . . . the eggwhite surrounding a ball of yellow lying together in an encased interior filled to the brim and fully intact, a perfect fit, with a little blood mark, a faint reddish tinge perhaps. The world is littered with eggs at Easter, but it is never enough just to hold one. With a dull thud against the side of a bowl the brittle shell cracks in two around its middle.

Remember Marj.

Remember Marj . . . her chooks and her fat brown fingers . . . and the way she cracked an egg and separated the two liquid parts by dribbling the thick part of the egg—the yellow eye—from one half shell to the other while the albumen dropped in a gob. She kept the yolk floating in a little milk for later, for when the eggwhites were whipped stiff. By looking into the fat eye, it is possible to ponder on what that fragile beginning of all things *stands* for, winging

11

its way from the past . . . It's always there . . . the cakes and tarts, eating and walking and then eating again, the washing and brushing away of flies, *her* hugs and drinking hot tea, cooking with a combination of sugar and eggs and milk, letting *him* touch (yes, that was part of the egg), then eating and watching the fingers curl, partaking in their embrace, this heart . . . an egg broken in two . . . the yellow eye staring . . .

The three eat their way south. "Do you know *anything* about where you're taking us, Mum?" asks Kate. The car is full of fruit. A box of mangoes and custard apples sits between the two girls on the back seat of the old Chrysler. There's a sharp stumpy knife for cutting the fruit, and pillows and blankets ready for concealing it all at the border. In the glove box, organically grown lemons of various shapes, sizes and colour threaten to burst the lock and litter the car. At the girls' feet lie the nearly forgotten pawpaws Sarah rescued from the bonnet. They eat avocado sandwiches for lunch, tea and supper, slicing the fruit in two around the hard brown seed, then carving half moon shapes in green and yellow through to the skin, ready to lie them flat between squares of fresh rye bread with a sprinkle of salt and pepper. Thick slices of mango and torn clumps of custard apple cleanse and sweeten their mouths before they bed down to sleep.

It is possible to live, I mean to *live*, in the past.

Molly's thoughts merge into dreams.

To *live*, don't you think Marj? I'm coming Marj, I'm coming home, with my two girls.

October 1960

In Molly Rose's dream the bed poured with a sea of thick creamy milk. The sticky wet worms fed off one another, breast deep. The strong ones grew fat.

At nine in the morning precisely, in a small registry office in the heart of London, Jimmy Brown married Molly Rose Moone. The year was 1960. They packed separately in the afternoon and slept in single beds on their wedding night at the bride's mother's home.

"You will write, won't you dear?" the mother asked.

"Yes Mummy, often, of course."

"You will tell me the *good news* first, dear."

"Yes Mummy."

"The layette's ready."

The day after the wedding, the newly-weds left for Australia from Waterloo Station. Everyone cried. Joyce Moone wept openly, shouting, "Tell me how big the sky is when you get there!" Jimmy and his new wife held hands, gloved and sweaty. The station smelt of grime and smoke and the London sky hung over their heads in a stagnant grey sac.

Jimmy Brown, the adventurer, had learnt about Australia from a window display. He read about the possibilities of migration, return passages, the miracle of ten pounds and Nest Egg arrangements for newly-weds with £500. He collected migrant brochures.

Jimmy wooed Molly Rose Moone. All that summer he followed her, making plans, with visions of a sun-drenched country bursting with opportunities, possibilities of a good job and a home filled with happy children. He turned his best side to her, all the while mulling over the arrangements in his mind.

Australia Offers

1960 Summer Passage
NEST EGG SCHEME
£10 gets you there
(children free)

She fell into his hand: a young purple fruit looking for distraction, for ripening and an escape from home. His gaze made her body pink, flushed; the greedy look he gave her in the florist's as she bought bouquets of white tulips for her mother. It was as if they were alone in the shop, Jimmy's green and yellow mismatched eyes smothering her body. She flickered from one coloured eye to the other, dreamily, the green more green because of the yellow, the yellow a shade of green, the colours deepening with growing size. His eyes alighted on her face with sheer absorption and thirst.

"Cc–cc–coffee," Jimmy said, stumbling through the words, pulling his ear lobe, eyes slit all of a sudden. These eyes were strong before he spoke, full moons, not crescents. But as he stuttered with his proposal it seemed that his face could be blown away. All she would need was a puff of air. "With me . . . n–now . . ." he pleaded and Molly Rose yielded.

Molly Rose learnt about Australia from Jimmy. He was thirty-four when they met, six foot six inches tall, with long legs in white pressed linen pants with wide cuffs. He told her he was a scientist, a soil scientist—she knew little about it— back home from an aborted trip to Africa. It hadn't worked out, the group he was with didn't get on and he was recu- perating, deciding what to do next. When he was thinking hard about something his tortoiseshell glasses would slip to the end of his nose before he pushed them back, abruptly. She thought him handsome. He had dark hair, and always a fleck of colour peeking from the top suit pocket. Colour was his god. As a seamstress, she was impressed.

"We'll ssss–see a l–lot of c–c–c–colour in Australia. It's a rr–rr–rock. S–something c–certain. Like my work, I ca–ca–n't do without. There's a l–l–ot of soil in Australia. Australia!" He smiled. Jimmy had no difficulty saying Australia. It was as if he were rehearsing for a stage production, with triumph in his voice. "I've always wanted t–t–to gg–ggo to Australia."

Jimmy Brown's stutter came in waves. Molly Rose ignored it, poised, caught up first with the repeating consonants and silence, then the colour in his face, the pulling of his ear lobes and whistling through wide-gapped teeth. She waited while he agonized over the position of his tongue, getting the teeth and jaw in the right place, corralling the lost syllables in a dry mouth.

He told her: "It's the position of the c–c–colour on the body, that t–tells, that says so much about a p–p–person."

She liked the music of his voice, his struggle for sounds and words. She thought it becoming, and listened as still as a cat basking in the sun, not really understanding him all of the time, but content to wait in anticipation of the final effect. It was the same as learning to make a new dress or watching her mother ice a cake, greedily, wanting to see how other people managed, how they did things, looking for satisfaction in the finished article, believing in dreams of others.

Her attraction to him could have been the way he looked and dressed, the way he spoke, but it was more. He appreciated her as an adult. He liked her being by his side, as if she replaced something missing from his past. And as they grew to know each other, even in the early days, Jimmy relaxed enough to talk without a stutter for a time. Then, he was able to speak in a smooth, liquid way Molly Rose would never have thought possible. It took her by surprise, perhaps disappointed her a little in the way it changed him in that instant from someone she adored into a stranger. And it was on one of these occasions over high tea at his flat, as he poured her a cup, that Jimmy told Molly Rose she reminded him of his mother. She loved to make clothes too, he said, cutting quite a figure in her day. Was it what he remembered, or what he'd dreamt his mother was like, for she died when he was a boy. He grew up then seeing her everywhere, on the streets and in shops and on buses, only to be disappointed each time as he drew close to the woman he followed. With Molly Rose, he said, it had been different. As he told her this, laying his hand over hers, there was a wistful look in his eye and a tug of a smile at the corner of his mouth, while she half-wished he'd kept the story to himself.

On the night of the Browns' marriage and on the eve of their journey across the world, while Jimmy snored loudly behind shut doors in the back room, Mrs Moone and her daughter sat on the floor in the lounge, counting and calculating, shifting piles of clothes and linen and household effects as well as Jimmy's field kit and books around the ten pieces of luggage. They whispered instructions to each other, arguing over what to take and the things to leave behind. Molly Rose insisted on including a trunk of material and her sewing machine.

"You'll never work with a child you know," Joyce said in reprimanding voice.

Without listening, however, Molly Rose packed her sewing box full of threads and bobbins and needles and buttons. Her work was important, and Jimmy said he understood. He reassured her she'd be able to keep on working in Australia, especially armed with fabrics she had collected, and finished samples of her London work.

"I'll get work Mummy," she said, closing the lid. "And if I do, I can send you a little money. I won't forget."

Joyce's pet pigeon bounced on his perch in time with their conversation. He was the last of her flock, the smallest, and lived in a big wire cage in a corner of the lounge. He'd never flown: his wings were clipped. Named after the colour of his feathers and the way they shone in a silky way under artificial light, Fudge let out little cooing noises, croo-croo, croo-croo, as if disturbed.

"Fudge, leave us alone will you. You'll miss him Rosy, you'll miss him. Look out for any pigeons, won't you. Tell me if they keep birds there. I don't know who I'll get to look after him when you're gone. I can't you know, I'm too old." And then as if resigned to her daughter leaving, she said, "It's time for bed now dear, an early start for us all tomorrow."

Waterloo Station, then Southampton docks. Wooden strutted gangplanks straddled a thin strip of deep water. With his eyes on the ship rather than down at the water, Jimmy carried the cabin bags a step ahead of his wife, her gloved hand grasping the rope rail. They kept close, in time with each other, and, while the other passengers waved coloured scarves from the crowded decks to farewell the motherland, Jimmy and Molly Rose made themselves comfortable below deck. Travelling by ship was a test for Jimmy, he said it was each time he went abroad, for he hated the water, it made him sick. "It'll be d–d–different having you though," he suggested, and she smiled reassuringly. At that moment the ship's horn let out a deafening blast that made the floor beneath their feet shudder.

"Rosy are you all right?" Jimmy asked that first night. They stood together in a corridor of full light. Stewards wandered past with their eyes averted carrying trays of glass and clinking ice balanced on their hands. She liked him calling her by the family's pet name. It made her grow large with affection. "R–R–Rosy I'll s–s–see you in the morning then," he added, "Here, s–s–s–omething before we g–g–o. A p–p–peck." Jimmy spat the word out. What courage he'd felt as he stood beside her, his new wife, deserted him all too quickly. "T–t–till morning then," his trousers quivered, "I'll s–see you th–th–, in the morning," Jimmy stammered it out, tongue pressed against his tonsils. He caught her hand in his, his fingers now cold and clammy, his eyes greedy for more, for something out of reach. Their hands fingered each other as if touching for the first time, not as honeymooners. He said a quick goodbye before turning his back to her.

She shut out the light and leaned against the wooden cabin door, sweat dripping over the skin of her stomach, and swayed with the gentle movement of the ship.

Molly Rose shared her cabin with eight other women for the six weeks of the voyage. She managed to secure a top bunk next to the porthole, for none of the other women were game. Outside, a watery world drifted past, and for comfort, the young woman watched the moon through her porthole. At times there lay a silvery path across the black water, so white and so certain she imagined she could walk on it to safety.

Jimmy slept squeezed into a crowded cabin on the bottom deck, below the water line, flat along the hull. He didn't sleep well, afraid his snoring might disturb the others, but it was more to do with the water. To pass the time he read the novels and biographies he'd packed, over and over again, deep into the night and until the early hours of the morning. Without Molly Rose, one of a kind in the cabin, he'd turn his back on the talk and jest and camaraderie of the other men and read. He said the stories helped keep his mind off the thought of the water and the memories of his beautiful mother who died, drowned, when he was a boy: Ethel Brown was never far from the surface. When he told Molly Rose this, she didn't know how to respond, wishing, again, he'd keep his thoughts to himself.

Every second night, the young and hopeful Molly Rose dressed herself in blue satin ready for dancing, tucking her small breasts behind sparkling sequins. Jimmy would invariably arrive late and stand at the doorway to the ballroom for a time, awkwardly, watching, looking for his wife. To match her gown, he wore his pressed black linen suit with a blue silk handkerchief in the pocket. He was thoughtful in this, but didn't know how to dance. So they passed away these evenings together sitting side by side in armchairs, on the edge of the dance floor, her toes tapping in time with the strings. Jimmy held Molly Rose's hand, rather tightly, while she sipped a vodka and orange through a swirled paper straw with a cigarette from the ship's supply between her fingers for support. Together they watched other young couples in tulle and taffeta and black tailored suits spiral around the polished wooden dance floor, their limbs interlocked, their lips creased in smiles.

a new picture

JIMMY GREW confident as they neared their destination. He'd read all about Canberra, as much as he could lay his hands on, and felt it beckoning. What better choice of home was there for a hopeful migrant and his wife, than a nation's burgeoning bush capital? Jimmy said he was ready to make a mark on the soil, carve out a decent profile as well as a name.

As an older woman Molly is going back to that place of adventure—the car is full of the aroma of fruit as her daughters sleep. *It is possible to live in the past*—she knows! Her spirit has fed off the masses of memories that multiplied in the fertility of a Queensland climate (Marj's original home of course), making her want to live, to give back . . . perhaps . . . If the girls were to ask her then, the reason for the sudden journey, she would have to make up an excuse, say, to visit the new Parliament House nearing completion, that mighty mini-city (or catacombs as some call it) being buried on Capital Hill with the best soil profiles for that area (Jimmy would know about it). No, no, it was more, but she couldn't tell them just yet . . . She could say it was out of curiosity (a faint smudge of redness in the eggwhite), to dip a finger into a lapping lake she'd not met, or to feel the fountain's spray across the bridge when the wind blows from the east (all the brochures have pictures). But she wouldn't be able to tell them it was to touch her, to be seduced again, to feel the power of that body . . . Ah, Molly sighs.

In 1960, Canberra lay in bits and pieces across the limestone plain either side of the Molonglo River. The newly-wed couple arrived before their luggage on a hot weekend in mid-November, just before the expected cool change. The capital of Australia was bare, dry and brown, mostly paddock, ordered in circles, loops and spirals, and very hot. They were both dizzy and disoriented by the time the taxi stopped in front of a brick house. It was tucked into the side of Mount Ainslie, on a big block, hedged at the front and fenced around the back. Semi-furnished and with modern amenities. Tree seedlings waiting in the shed were wrapped in damp newspaper and bound with green garden string: the makings of a garden, given ten or more years.

On arrival they stood together on the front drive mesmerized and speechless, dizzy with fatigue and heat, swishing the flies away from their faces with a brush, brush, brush of their hands. It was the only movement. Stillness all around.

Molly Rose was first in, up the three concrete steps and through a flapping fly door, her legs heavy and aching, shoes off, to have a quick flick through the rooms. Her stockinged feet skated over the coolness of the linoleum. The double brick walls shunned the heat. Each room housed the barest of furniture.

The lounge overlooked the front garden, a large square of grass with a late spring flicker of growth amongst the dry winter covering, bone brown interspersed with lime green. She slipped off her greasy bracelet-length gloves and pressed her hand against the pane of glass with its faint smell of methylated spirits. She stood close to the window, gazing outside. Out there, tall smoky green and washed-brown eucalypts stood to attention, scribbled statues against the purples, greys, blues and pinks of a mountain range in the distance. Molly Rose had never seen mountains like these. She wondered what grew on them, whether the spell would be broken if she went closer and touched their flanks.

That night a neighbour brought the newcomers food— tinned meat, cucumber sandwiches and glasses of cold beer amongst everything else. More than enough for an evening meal. She'd breezed into the kitchen unannounced. "So you're the English lot." A chance meeting you could say. Fresh, unexpected, spontaneous. Everything Molly Rose's upbringing told her to guard against.

The neighbour looked at them questioningly as the young Englishwoman stumbled over their names, covering for her husband, saying Jimmy and Molly Rose all at once, forgetting to say Brown.

"What's that, Jimmy and Molly, lovely, you'll fit in, well, you've come on a beauty. Cool change's due soon. Hottest day this season. Never so early and as it's only November, we're in for a stinker come February. Take a while to get used to I suppose, never trying a shift from cold to hot myself, been brought up in Queensland you know, but don't mind me, I've brought you some tea. Nothing's worse than arriving some place new and the shops are shut, they're miles away anyway and it's hot, you're tired and you've come all the way from across the other side of the world, to Canberra, the best-lit paddocks in Australia! Or as some say, you know the turkeys from the coast who think they own the place when it comes to cities, the biggest garden outside a city. At least it's got a garden, and the trees are the best part. Just you wait, this place will be the envy of Australia, mark my word!"

The newcomers stood transfixed on the other side of the kitchen, against the red and white flecked bench top. They leaned heavily, watching the woman bustle confidently around the room. They struggled to keep up with what she was saying, without even knowing her name. How could they interrupt politely? Jimmy licked his lips, shining wet and pink, and pulled at his navy dot tie, pushing his chin from side to side, loosening his jaw, wondering how they could get rid of her without being rude. Molly Rose smiled weakly, craning her head forward, neck extended, eyes dilated, curious and wondering at the huge woman who talked, her body fluttering with each word.

"I've only brought this, you can keep it for the kitchen till all your belongings arrive, they can take time I know and I can lend you other bits and pieces as you need." She dumped a picnic hamper onto the square table in the middle of the kitchen. "I've already put some old blankets and sheets on the big bed, although you'll only need a sheet to cover you tonight. Jeez it's hot. We're used to migrants around here."

Molly Rose coughed and Jimmy stomped his foot, involuntarily. The fluorescent tube crackled; its flood of light wobbled. A flypaper suspended from the ceiling swayed, with yet another victim struggling to free itself.

"Not that I mind, mind you. Australian-born myself, but there's English blood in my great-grandmother, well Irish if the truth be known. Through and through. See, I've got some cucumber sandwiches because you're English and I wanted to make you feel at home. There's camp pie—you open it yourself with a silver key on the bottom of the tin— and sausages, lettuce with a mayonnaise dressing (I use Keen's mustard myself to give it a spark), cold cooked potatoes, jellied beetroot squares, lemon meringue pie and a thermos of hot milky tea, and oh, cold beer for you . . ." the woman stared at Jimmy's parted pink lips, "To finish off with. Hope it's to your liking."

She unpacked a basket of plates, cutlery and cups in matching hard red plastic.

"The basket was a wedding present, I've filled it with picnic things because we haven't used it much really, we never go on picnics, Kev's not interested, oh that's the old man," she continued breezily, filling the flecked bench top with food. She stood the thermos on its end and leaned the empty basket against the food safe's flyscreen.

"Oh, by the way, for a welcoming touch," and the neighbour went to place a jar of small beady flowers in the centre of the low coffee table in the dining room. "They're from around here. I thought you might like that, to see what's here really. They don't smell that good but I love the colour. Late spring flowers." And as an afterthought, more to the woman of the house, she said, "I'll take you to the bush one day, walk in it, smell it, tread on it, our virgin land. Then you'll not be afraid of anything, you'll see."

With that she was gone.

They didn't have to say a word.

But before either could move, the woman poked her head around the back door again. "If you need anything Molly, I'm next door. Anything at all, I'd love to help." She winked at her, sending goose bumps down the Englishwoman's spine. Quite unexpected. "I'm from next door and I'm Marj. Marj Waters."

Molly (for that's what she suddenly decided to call herself after hearing her name on the lips of this astonishing person) watched the space in the door, expecting Marj to emerge again, to fill it all a third time. She was both drawn to the new neighbour and slightly repulsed by her abruptness and size and ease of place.

And years later, it was with the same elements that Molly felt caught out again, even challenged. Marj could emerge at any time.

Later, in the week before Easter in 1988, Molly had begun the morning unsure of where it would all end. While she groped about in the half-light, Jimmy's letter from the day before nibbled at her mind's lining. His words wouldn't let her go: *You mean a lot to me* . . . She was in a whirl. By that time Molly had lived in Queensland for over twenty years, and the Sunshine Coast had become her favourite stamping ground. She knew the beaches well, those zips of luxury threading together two realities. But it was Mudjimba she was thinking of, the Old Woman. Separated out from the land, alone. She'd been introduced to the island before, of course, the lump of land fading in and out of sight depending on the weather. If only she had had a clear sense of destiny, then she'd be smiling at the thought of the forthcoming meeting. She'd taken the Chrysler to her favourite beach, the one north of the Maroochy River channel and close to the airport, along the esplanade, and then back south down North Shore Road. Unurbanized, this stretch of sand was protected by a recreational reserve. A little wild, this small piece of natural bushland in a development-crazy coastline was the perfect place for private nude bathing.

Out at sea, the island lies low in the water, the island her daughter Kate says she wants to go scuba diving around.

Molly walked with her head down much of the way, her hands more relaxed than at the beginning, Jimmy's letter and boronia clasped together. As she turned to trace her way back up the face of the dune to where the car was parked, something caught her attention, a tug of a loose thread. She paused. And as she stared out to sea, the small island offshore drifted in and out of her consciousness, overlaying her thoughts with its form. The Old Woman, Mudjimba. Then in an instant Molly's face lit up with recognition. How could she have been so careless? Mudjimba was none other than her Marj, a cushion of rock lying low in a caressing body of water, well supported from fathoms below. And she'd been there all the time, in all weathers, without Molly really seeing. A physical reality, not a dreaming.

Marj beckoned.

It was after that sighting, while riding the bumps home in the Chrysler with its floating liquid motion, that Molly confirmed her decision. Putting a face to Mudjimba had clinched it. She would pack immediately to leave the next morning.

That night Jimmy and Molly sat either side of the coffee table with Marj's posy of flowers as a centre-piece, eating a supper of potato and cucumber sandwiches. In a trance and not wanting to be rude, they overate—finishing off as much as they could. The dessert had to be left untouched. The milky tea was piping hot, burning Molly's throat as she rinsed down her food. Jimmy poured his beer down the drain in the kitchen sink.

Neither of them mentioned Marj all evening, *she* could tell *he* didn't want to. While Molly showered, Jimmy distanced himself further with fluent words spoken through the bathroom door. He said, "I expect there are *some* English people here in Canberra. Australia is full of them. That's why we came wasn't it? A little England over the other side of the world. We'll find them, Rosy, and feel completely at home. T–t–trust me." Jimmy faltered only at the end.

"Jimmy, call me Molly from now on, please," she shouted back. "I think it suits me." She wasn't interested in finding

England in Australia. She wanted the real thing, delighted with her first encounter.

"But you're Mo–Mo–M–olly R–R–R–Rose, surely," Jimmy struggled with her name. "R–R–Rosy!"

"See, even *you* find it hard to say . . ." she said, the hot steam giving her some protection. "I'm sorry, that's unfair, but truly, I didn't think it would be like this, I think it will just be easier that's all. I'm starting in a new place and I want to do it properly. I'm *going* to be *Molly*!" The water thundered hot and cold. "This shower's a waterfall. It goes everywhere! And there's no curtain." She drowned any reply of his with the roaring noise.

She was drawn to Marj, her voice and ease of place, even if Jimmy wasn't. It was as if Marj had always been here, wearing the country in and over her skin like a dress. Some people wore clothes that didn't fit or suit them. They were too large or too small, the wrong colours, inappropriate texture and length, or too fashionable and not in keeping with their age and body line. There were others who knew how to wear what they chose instinctively. Naturals. And Marj had it! She carried it—this something. No fuss. Marj belonged. For that reason, this newcomer wanted to see more. And she wanted to be known as Molly—Molly Brown.

"These blinds won't c–c–c–ome down. I want p–privacy." Jimmy interrupted her thoughts in a loud voice. "I'm co–c–c–oming in soon."

Molly knew he wouldn't shower with her; join her on the square concrete dip in the floor, naked and wet without a curtain. Jimmy would come into the bathroom and watch, fully clothed and dry. Later, when she was gone and wrapped in a towel, or clothed in her nightie, he would wash alone, hurriedly, with the doors locked. A dip, not a soak.

On the ship, the separate living quarters had suited him. Only in the final week did Jimmy break the rules to satisfy his craving by sneaking up to Molly's cabin on the higher deck, to observe her showering. With the coast clear he'd wrapped his body in the floral rubberised curtain dividing the small cream cubicles, his black hair wet and limp over his forehead, glasses fogged with steam, watching her skin colour with heat from the water. Jimmy thought she didn't know—his entrance was silent and her back turned. He stood on tiptoe, his black leather lace-ups wet from the splash. A miniature reflection in the chrome shower attachment above her squeezed his features. And an oversized shadow cast by the light on the opposite wall dominated the reflective tiles, his head out of proportion with his body. Molly laughed, as if about something unrelated, loving the feel of her body, enjoying his feasting eyes on her figure, growing used to him looking and accepting his perversity without question. Accepting this as marriage.

"Well, w–w–welcome to Australia," Jimmy said. There he was, filling the doorway of their new bathroom, legs and arms crossed, his mouth suppressing a gasp, intent on giving nothing away. "Your first shower. Can I stand here?" His head hung low as he pulled at his ear pretending he was seeing her for the first time—her titillative bareness— but his eyes gave him away. Anyway his sentence was clean, betraying a confidence. He blushed, pushing his glasses up his nose.

She turned her back to him and glimpsed a moon's crescent through the bathroom louvres. The November night sky was in evening dress, in black velvet with diamantine points, and the young moon danced, brushing against the clouds in a waltz. Different country. Same moon. Molly wondered whether Marj had a bathroom like theirs, with a slide frame window projecting a picture of this dance through slithered glass.

The water ran hot over her body, her skin red with heat.

a question of timing

ON THE first morning she lay in the makeshift double bed (Jimmy had slept on the floor in the next room), a sheet tucked in and pulled to her chin, staring at the long shafts of light which caught the dust. She was dazzled by the brightness of the sun. She was trying to visualize her neighbour again.

Jimmy had left early to explore the town and buy provisions. He said as he went, "D–on't know when I'll be b–back. Don't wander t–too far." He adjusted his tie while staring at her sleeping body. "Don't get t–too involved too s–s–oon."

Molly kept her eyes closed. Unflickering lids.

"That w–woman . . . d–d–don't get t–t–too involved will you?"

Acrobatic flies spun and flipped in midair.

Molly answered with silence.

And dreamt of open spaces and THE PLAN: to meet her neighbour again.

Plans don't always work out. Why is she taking the girls all the way to Canberra for such a short time? They will ask questions for sure, especially Kate, she wants to know every-thing. What's the point? she'll say. And what's the interest all of a sudden? If Molly is to give a straightforward, single-line answer, it will be this: she can't see Jimmy until she sees Marj first. But how does she know Jimmy? Who's Marj? And Sarah will put her arm around Molly, hold her tight. She is the quieter, more supportive twin. She'll do anything to make her mother happy.

On the night before leaving Queensland and the flat filled with ocean debris collectibles, the air was calm but thick. Tropical humidity clings to the body like a second skin, and sweat trickles as a caution. A blessing and a curse. No more so than that night in late March, one hundred or so kilo-metres north of Brisbane, past the Glasshouse Mountains of Beerwah and Beerburrum, in Maroochydore, the heart of the Sunshine Coast. Molly opened the windows and sliding doors onto the small balcony in order to snare wisps of movement. The sea breeze had come and gone earlier in the evening. She lay on top of her bottom sheet, naked, face down in the shape of a cross, her limp arms stretched either side, her toes searching the cotton surface for cool patches. And still she sweated. The light of the city threw an uneasy corn colour across the bed and her bareness. It was the night she dreamt of a sea of thick milk, the white and sticky worms, all rigid, quite still.

Restless, she woke early. She'd be seeing Marj soon. That was the answer to the question wasn't it, of why she was going south? But it's never as simple as that. In the beginning God made Adam and Eve, and it was very good, in plan. *Tell me the old, old story*. Or at least that's what the Bible says (Marj never believed a word!). Perfection, if that's what you're searching for, is a matter of timing; a matter of knowing when to eat the fruit in your hand.

But she wasn't to know that back then, in the beginning. Instead . . .

She hadn't been able to sleep that first night in Canberra.

Jimmy slept deeply, snored heavily.

And the outside mysterious world beckoned.

She would never dream of doing such a thing in England, there'd be no point with the sky heavy like unleavened dough. But here, with a velvet evening sky tantalizing her senses, she felt strangely safe, enticed even, to draw the brunch coat more closely, and to step lightly down the two back steps, dressed for a ball.

The moon she had met earlier in the shower shone behind a flicker of cloud. Rings of colour circled the white curve. The sky looked so close yet distant all at once, the air thick enough to shake hands with. A wooden paling fence marked out the suburban block boundary, one side vacant, the other Marj's garden. There was something comforting about a well-defined square, a private view of the flaunty sky and the bush beyond the back fence. She made a vow to climb over the back fence eventually, in daylight, and to explore the virgin land, rustling and creaking with shadows, the tall trees and shrubs rising to something of a mountain behind in a mirror image of the mysterious range beyond the town's limit. And maybe, in time, to climb the shared fence into her neighbour's garden.

Her garden was uneven and bare, with a shed in the corner, a tree, and a washing line—a steel spider's web perched horizontally on a thick post planted in cement. This much she could see in the dark. Six squares of concrete lay in a rough path from the back door to the foot of the post, the spider's precarious home. Molly imagined hanging her washing on the spirals of the silver web and winding the load up high with the handle. It looked manageable, not so exposed in the dark. Comfortable. She went to the empty line, and pushed the cross-wires around and around with the tips of her fingers, till it whirred . . .

It was then, with the line twirling in full flight, freely and openly and her mind filling it with sloppy wet washing, that she heard a voice, enticing and ethereal, and so clear

31

with acoustic precision, it was as if she were standing in a
darkened cathedral. She stopped her imaginary washing,
listening, entranced.

Drifting from next door, the gramophone didn't crackle,
for that's what she thought it was at first. It hummed.

Then a woman's voice shouted: "You can never wait, can
you?"

There was a long pause, followed by laughter.

"Bloody impatient. Yes I *know* you go tomorrow. I'll be
with you soon."

"Stop tickling. Kev!!"

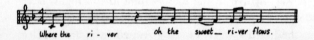

She imagined Marj in the bathroom—for that's who it *had* to be—mouth open in song—she could hear bubbles of water in the notes—with the falling water a continuo, her body a well-proportioned speaker, vibrating with the deep voice, muscles loose but full of music, and Kev—a shadowy attachment—tickling her body to make it contort and ripple, his fingers practised in pleasure.

So Kev—Kev?—would be gone in the morning. Eavesdropping made her a little hot. For how long? With prickling skin. Maybe enough time for her to see Marj again, to begin a conversation, to hear her talk. She wanted to see Marj alone, and settled in her mind that the washing would be the way to begin (*Where the river oh the sweet river flows*), for from the line she could see into their garden. Yes, standing on tiptoe, blushing at being so bold, she saw her friend had a spider's web too. It shone in the soft moonlight. They couldn't help spotting each other, in time.

At home, her mother cleaned and cooked. Joyce Moone hung everything above the meat stews and boiling potatoes in the kitchen. It was the driest place for wet washing. The lines crisscrossed the ceiling. Through her pubescent years, Molly remembered her mother hanging blood-stained napkins above the stews in the kitchen (menstruation *was* a curse), and later, bras and step-ins. She learnt to duck her head, avoiding drips. The kitchen was private territory, guests relegated to the front rooms, for Joyce considered it obscene to handle and view underclothes outside the family. Because of the lack of space, large items were kept to a minimum. They were dried in clumps, folded back on themselves, and kept for weeks. They always smelt damp and looked grey.

On the ship, Molly had thrown an occasional piece of dirty but respectable clothing into the cabin's washing basket. It came back folded neatly and ironed. Unable to throw off the habits of home, she washed her underwear by hand, and hung it up to dry on the bed rail overnight. The extraordinary heat of the cabins dried synthetics in minutes, while cotton bras and corsets took longer and held the smell of stale food in the woven fibres. With warmth and time on her hands in Canberra, however, and the possibility of seeing Marj again, the silver line would whirr, full of clothes, her clothes, Jimmy's clothes . . . on second thoughts, she decided to peg up the safest washing on the outside, sorting the laundry into *big* and *small*, *outsides* and *insides*. Their private pieces would be kept for the kitchen (her mother would be proud).

Anyway that was the plan.

The lights of Marj's house shone brightly in the darkness.

dress looked light and crisp, but she felt naked, not ready for the feel of bare arms and legs and an open square neck. The pleats swam around her thighs, licking her skin, so she pulled on a pink step-in and rolled a thin pair of stockings up her warm legs so as to feel comfortable and more normal. She straightened the back seam and clipped the tops to her suspender belt. As an afterthought, she added a lace half-slip as another protective layer.

She looked at herself in the bathroom mirror with its scalloped edge and frosted corner flowers and touched her pale skin with pink rouge, her body secure now, firm and held together. Trying to be objective, she imagined Marj looking at her, seeing what she would see, and curled her lip in surprise. As a final touch and in order to calm herself, she coloured those lips again, with more deep red. She was ready.

With a triangle of leftover cucumber sandwich in one hand, Molly opened the fly door at the back, her senses heightened with the thought of her beguiling neighbour. She stood for a long time in the doorway, squinting into the glare of the day.

On her escapade the night before, the sky had been close and comforting, a neat black evening cloak. Now, with the sun up, it was more like a huge mouth yawning, the blueness disappearing up the back of its throat, waiting to gobble her up. The garden looked smaller, the bush tall behind, and her washing line dominated. She would have to be careful sorting the clothes.

Marj's washing was already on her line (the view was good from the back step), a jumble of different clothes in no particular order flapping in the morning breeze. A fresh paling fence, chest high, separated the two gardens. Its golden timber glowed like honey in the sun. The neighbour's garden, three times as long as Molly's, with a chicken house in the far corner, was full of plants. Unknown bushes and trees as well as familiar flowers decorated newly raked beds.

As a centre-piece to the garden, a focus to the eye, there was a bird-bath carved out of pink stone. Molly had never seen one as large or as ornate as this. It was quite beautiful but seemed slightly out of place, as if it didn't belong. Even more surprising was the way a brilliant scarlet and blue bird with long tail feathers landed on its rim for a drink, then in a flash disappeared.

Molly crossed her arms; she felt joy in her heart.

She would write home and tell her mother all about it: the bush, the bird-bath of pink stone, the bird, the sky. She remembered Joyce's last words spoken through the open carriage door as it edged out of Waterloo Station, her mother's face alight with excitement at her daughter's daring adventure. It was to do with the sky: Tell me how big the sky is, she said. In a shout Joyce had added with her hands cupped around her mouth for better projection, the noise of the snaking train nearly drowning the words, "Let me know if pigeons would like it?" With a first good view of the yawn above, Molly imagined her mother's tagged pigeons—the ones she used to have bunched up in their cages stacked one on top of the other in the small garden—flying around in speckled circles and V's across Canberra, dipping behind the now-visible mountain at the back of their house, then veering across the town to the far range, black swirling dots against a wash of blue and white colour. Somehow they would make this sky seem closer, more real and tangible. Her mother's old pigeons would help define the yawn and Molly wouldn't get lost, sucked up into an eternity.

But what about those native birds? Those splashes of colour? Molly would write home immediately to tell Joyce there wasn't room for domestic birds, and her mother would never make the long journey to check. As she thought of this, she was surprised not to feel any regret, loss or home-sickness for her mother, or for the tagged flying V's, the strays catching up with the flock she used to love to watch, circling the grey skies as a child.

It was simple. Everything here belonged to her. What's more, a wide open land with its full body circumscribed by the famous beaches she longed to see and then an ocean beyond that, lay between this newness and home. Her legs wobbled a little, her gaze cavorting and skipping about the empty sky. Turning to go in, she was ready now to get on with the washing. As she did so she noticed an unused wooden gate, crowded with green tangled creepers, at the end of the fence line separating the two gardens. It was a gate into Marj's rambling garden. How odd but how pleasing! So she wouldn't have to learn to climb the fence after all. Immediately she felt a powerful sensation of desire, although she couldn't name it. It made her quivery and hot, unbalanced and bare.

land of the big sky

EARLY SUMMER skies over Canberra were bottomless blue and puffed by gentle winds. Boundless stable weather lapped and dipped over the horizon. Anything would dry in a morning.

At first Molly kept to the shade of her house. She felt more comfortable in under the eaves; a step away from her new kitchen but with a view to Marj's garden. There, she waited impatiently for a glimpse of Marj (the woman had to bring in her washing sometime). Molly's first day turned out to be uneventful, useless, without so much as a whispering acknowledgement of the neighbour's presence. And two loads of washing were wasted, two loads of safe bedding. In the small rectangular laundry, Molly stood over the Whirlpool wringer washing machine perched on the cement floor on a set of castors, running through the whole operation. She soaped and sloshed about and wrung out all manner of things, pillowcases, sheets, tea-towels and bed protectors. She turned the knob on the side of the tub to stop the agitator, then pushed the wet washing through the cream rubbery cylinders of the wringer, catching them on the other side with a free hand. The linen rolled out as thin pastry, folding back on itself in a looping pile.

On the second day, Jimmy started out early again. He went to the used car yards to look for a suitable car they could afford. They would purchase an *Australian* motor car, he'd decided (he hadn't commented on the neighbours' Vanguard in their driveway). He wore his best black suit, with a scarlet handkerchief in the top pocket. Molly stayed at home and attacked the pile of leftovers from the day before, pleased with her efforts so far, but determined more than ever to meet Marj again. But Marj's washing was already out again by the time Molly's machine started up, so she gave up any hope of synchronizing the procedure with her neighbour. Another way would have to be found because all that was left to wash was the Browns' accumulated underwear, destined for a drying line strung out across the kitchen.

Molly got on with the job. She rinsed and wrung and rinsed and wrung and dumped the damp underclothes into a large cane basket, cradled in a frame on small wheels. The laundry was steaming with the hot water and her movement. Rows of beaded sweat appeared across her top lip. Her bare feet slipped over the smooth moist concrete. It was then, in the middle of it all, she heard the voice jumping at her. Arrested, Molly forgot to breathe.

"Yoo-hoo, anybody home?"

The wringer caught Molly's fingers as Marj's lumbering body and voice shadowed the laundry. Her cheeks hot, Molly turned to face the figure at the door, unable to say a word. Still holding a string of wet clothes in one hand, she flicked the other sore one automatically.

"Beat you to it didn't I? Mine's out already, flapping on the line. I'm Marj, do you remember me? From next door? Thought I'd just hop in to see how you're all going. I didn't want to be too nosy you know, so I've given you time to get settled. Lovely day for washing." Marj filled the doorway, her fat hands on round hips, her black hair plaited in a thick twirl around her head.

"Hello," Molly returned, breathing heavily and clearing her throat, then repeating it, with more vigour. She licked the sweat away with her tongue. "Hello. Yes. I'm Molly . . ." She caught herself midstream before confessing to the Rose part. Molly still sounded good she thought, like the first night. Much easier to roll off the tongue. She had spoken. Past the first hurdle.

"Molly, now that's a nice name, where are you from? Oh I know you're from the old country," not waiting for a reply and throwing her hands about with gesticulations, "But which part? Molly doesn't sound too English to me. But I wouldn't really know. I'm fourth generation Australian on one side, fifth on the other. We go back a long way. But nobody really admits that these days and for the life of me I don't know why. Afraid of a convict past or something."

Marj raced when she talked and Molly found it hard to keep up, not used to the speed, the thick accent and volume. When Marj paused for breath, everything else seemed to stand still for that small moment, listening, ready for the next clump of sentences. The air around Marj fairly snatched its own breath, taking stock quickly before the talking started again, for there wouldn't be time midstream. It was so unlike anything Molly was used to. Her mother was a good talker, slow and dense, but manageable. And Jimmy talked at a snail's pace. Over the time she'd known him, Molly had learned to wait, not for a small break, a gasp, a snatch between a string of sentences, but for one painful word.

"So, come and I'll help you. I'll help you with anything for that matter. I'm good to know because I've been living in these parts for a while, not that I feel completely at home. I'm not sure anyone does here, it's a funny sort of place really. It always has the feeling that everyone is waiting for something to happen, waiting to move on or for something to arrive. Like a platform at a railway station, going interstate, we're waiting for the train to arrive, or for more passengers to get off, trying to see someone we recognise, something like that anyway. Either that, or as if its heart never got here. All the different parts ordered, but somehow the heart was missing from the plan or it got stolen or lost and no one can find it, or it's not been invented yet! Ha, that's a joke isn't it? It'll come though; maybe when the lake goes in. It'll be a drawcard in the middle of the town, a focus, reason to be here, make it all pretty and irresistible and watery, lots of sport for the sporty ones—that sort of thing. Can't wait. At the moment, it's like a great big modern paddock in the middle of nowhere. Painfully dry and windswept—rain is something else here. Everyone wants to know about Canberra, because it's so important, to visit of course, but never live here. But you've had enough of me, let's get these clothes out before they dry stiff and awkward in the basket."

While Marj was talking, rocking her weight from foot to foot and keeping the flies away from her face with a rhythmical swishing of the hand, Molly had found it hard not to look at her skin. It was unlike anything she had seen.

Marj Waters was fat, but it wasn't only her bulk that interested Molly. It was the colour and texture of her skin— smooth and strong and brown. The skin was stretched, the fine body hair bleached, not mottled but hardened, good-looking, hard-working skin; skin she would feel proud to bare. She wondered how long it would take to get some for herself—muscles taut, hide dried out in warm air. How many hours basking in the sun, to become leather brown? And what did it feel like to have naked legs and arms coated with a colour and a lightness, a breeziness against the skin, a match to the air and colour and texture of the place itself? This skin was so different from the creamy paleness she carried, from the doughy sometimes blotchy skin she covered with cotton, or stocking silk on best occasions.

Molly Brown wanted to get into her neighbour's skin, clothe herself with it, feel its dryness and colour with clean cool fingers.

"Oh yes, of course, the washing, yes I've finished this bit." She jerked back to the present, wondering whether she'd ever be able to do it, get that skin.

"Come on I'll help you, we can talk outside while we're doing it." Marj was on her way out.

"Uhm, actually, I was going to hang these inside." Molly smiled awkwardly, remembering her sorting and the contents of the basket. "I've got a line in the kitchen."

"No, don't be silly, you don't hang anything inside on days like today. If you're afraid of the bleaching sun, then turn them inside out, hide all the good bits with pegs, the bits that fade, but don't stay indoors. There's no point when you're blessed with a hot drying sun like ours."

"Jimmy put it up especially last night."

But Marj was already out, she hadn't heard. Molly had no choice but to follow the fat swinging neighbour pushing her basket of clothes.

Had she not washed the day before, Molly wouldn't have minded Marj being with her to hang out the clothes: they would have strung up sheets and curtains and mattress protectors together, the English migrant unashamed and happy. She thought again of her basket, the looping flat piles —the telling underwear—hers and Jimmy's. She looked at Marj with her round face bordered with clipped kiss-curls, her skin and her fatness. A dirty-white petticoat strap hung down to her elbow on either side, carelessly. Her bosom bulged with buried handkerchiefs. Her feet flat, plump and bare. Toes splayed. She barely knew this woman, but sensed it was better that way. Marj needn't know about her anxieties, the way things are done in England, that her mother thinks handling underwear is rude and disgusting. Molly recalled the heavy skies she left behind and the damp grey washing coming off the line before the frost, on the good days. She looked at Marj again, who was talking, her open moon face pointing straight up to the pegs and the blue sky above.

"You know, this house has been empty for months," Marj was off again. "It's nice to have it filled now. Not good for the government to have houses wasted when there's such a to-do about shortages and waiting lists. You're very privileged you know, lucky to get into one as good as this, but I know you must have some money tucked away, you're no ordinary Ten Pounder. Don't be embarrassed, we get a lot around here, working on construction sites. They live in the hostels mainly, without families. It's rough for them. And you'll be staying for a good time, so it makes me feel more comfortable, just to know this house isn't empty. We need people coming here to stay." Marj's chatter eased Molly's mind. It was as if Marj didn't care what clothes she put out to dry. Everything had to be washed eventually, so everything had to dry outside.

"Come on, I'll give you a hand then we'll have a nice cup of tea."

Marj pushed the trolley closer and, working side by side with wooden dolly pegs, the two women pegged up the washing in rows. Marj pegged the clothes in such a matter-of-fact way, it was impossible for Molly not to follow suit. She forgot to blush.

"These are good drying days. Washing's a breeze on this line, like mine, everything dries so well, and it rotates as well, swings around in the wind. I'll show you all the tricks while you're here. Now, if there's anything at all you need, don't hesitate to ask, and I'll give you an answer or point you in the right direction." Marj pegged up the last pair of underpants. They hung with the crotch down, sagging and limp. "Come on Molly, come and have tea with me. It's the civilized thing to do in the morning now all the washing's out and you can tell me something about yourself . . ."

"Thanks, thanks ever so much, maybe another time, I have to go in now, other things to see to, other jobs, you know organizing things, setting them right, unpacking, thanks for your help." Molly found herself racing like Marj, to keep up, to fill the air with as much sound as her new neighbour. Having survived the washing, she wanted to stay with Marj, dearly, but the spell was broken. She craved the indoors again, the walls of her own house, wanting to digest the morning in private. In time she would have cups of tea with Marj. They would grow fond of each other, used to one another, intimate and close. She wanted it more than

45

anything else. She wanted to clothe herself with that skin.
Imitate Marj.

a flying V

LETTERS BETWEEN hemispheres form tangles of feeling: feelings of affection laced with misunderstanding, feelings of hope and desire mixed with disappointment, feelings of repulsion at the watery separation mingled with pleasure in the pinpointed distance. Personal, highly charged, there is something strangely intimate about the receiving, and at times giving, of letters. You carry the sheets of paper around with you, scrunched in a bag or a hand, or to mark the place in a book. You even sleep with them close to the body and they don't change their mind—until another instalment arrives, and even then you will always have the first to remind you. They are the still frame of a moving picture. And piece by piece you can thread the story together at your leisure, roll the film on.

Over the years of separation, Jimmy's letters marked his presence in her life for better and for worse, part of an unhealed sore, an irritation at times and yet, a pleasure too, where itching brings relief, where the itching becomes the pleasure, a kind of slow seepage, a liquidising of the hitherto concealed lump of desire within. This pleasure, this itching, the undissolved salts in the sand.

And it is one of Jimmy's letters that is making her go south. Jimmy of all people.

In 1960, letters took much longer to find a home. The pace of communication was slow. Letters crisscrossed from mother to daughter all that first summer in tangled, unconnecting lines, forming clumps of meaning in transit, on the

47

ships and airplanes, rather than at each end. Molly wrote to Joyce from the Brown's first night in Canberra onwards.

Dear Mummy, she wrote, *we've arrived. I forgot to tell you we had a wonderful bombe Alaska for my nineteenth birthday! What a scream. The lights went out, the blinds were drawn, and a line of waiters with blue flames swimming on silver dishes swept into the massive dining room. All the children cried in fear, and the orchestra played Happy Birthday. Afterwards everyone danced in the main hall and saloons, the music circling the ship in a cloud. I wore my blue satin ball gown with the sequins in a loop around the low neckline, you know the one that falls to the floor in a tear-drop . . . Canberra is so hot. The sky here is big, mountains purple and pink, Australians brown. The air is paper blue. Something to watch from the shade of our new house—it's a fine house, very generous. My eyes water with the heat . . . Love Molly*

The letters Molly wrote formed a lattice in her mind. She found them to be both a protection and a security, a means of making sense of the newness.

Dear Mummy . . . I've got a friend. She lives next door and she sings. Her name is Marj . . . Love MOLLY

She tied them up in her memory as she would the curling tendrils of a vine, feeding her own needs rather than her mother's, twirling the new growth neatly around events. The connections grew longer and faster as a result, doubling and tripling in size.

Those she received from Joyce Moone were full of her mother's favourite topics, mostly to do with pigeons and having a daughter. They reminded Molly of all she had left behind—an ageing mother, one whose tired body stooped to the ground, degenerating quickly with grief once she realized her only child had really gone. The letters were enjoyable to read, as good as instalments in a magazine, but Molly found it hard to feel an honest homesickness: she was too proud of her own bravery of migrating into the unknown.

She read her mother's erratic letters while sitting on the porch step. It overlooked the front garden bordered by its short clipped hedge and the smooth black bitumen road with concrete gutters beyond. The daughter enjoyed this long-distance conversation. No more close heavy breathing in a small house, face to face with awkward silences for replies. The oceans and continents between Australia and England fragmented their conversation, eased the tension, the sentences not meeting or making sense until way after the event. Entirely bearable, objective, rather comic.

Dear Rosy, Joyce wrote . . . *I can see for miles past the length of the balcony and gargoyle corners right over the tree tops. They're losing their leaves now it's cold. I am a bird. Sometimes I fly right out of the window . . .*

Joyce replied in the way she talked, slow and dense, with an eye for detail.

Dear Rosy, I am sitting up in bed and I feel completely here. When you were a child, you used to say that to me— "Mummy, I feel completely here." It was a lovely sentiment. Anyway—now—in this place, the covers are snowy white and starched, just lightly done, with a red stripe down the middle. The covers hang over the edge of the bed like a long hair cut, I hope Jimmy boy doesn't let his hair grow over his ears. He is such a nice boy, you are a lucky girl you know, it's not every nineteen-year-old who wins such a prize, I do hope he takes good care of you—oh by the way, that string of pearls can be for your birthday. My darling flower, don't let yourself be crushed. Glad to know you're there now. I can see it more clearly I had trouble with the ship not knowing where you were. Love Mummy xxx

Touching the string of pearls around her neck, Molly skimmed over the spidery words written in brown ink. Her mother's words failed to touch her deeply, but she couldn't do without them, even though over time the letters became muddled and repetitive and rambling, losing their clear focus.

. . . I leave a note in fountain ink on my bedside table, it reads: GONE FOR A GENTLE FLY BE BACK SOON. Pigeons always return Rosy and as I go I can smell them what a glorious glorious smell. Do tell me if there are any birds over there. I should love to know. The smell fills my nose and burns the back of the throat—just how it should—the neat countryside so wee below . . .

From her shaded perch on the front step, letter in hand, Molly gazed at her new naked garden, the pale hardsetting beds. The thought of the English countryside made her nostalgic for its green lawns, clipped to one inch exactly, all over, and the rows of traditional flowers in raised beds of moist dark earth. But then she remembered the vegetable soup skies, the soft rain watering the boggy marsh. What a contrast to where she was now. Australia grew at the back of their house, beyond the fence and up the flank of Mount Ainslie. It was full of powder-puff, acid yellow wattles and gums flowering in whites and creams and pinks, the ground covered with fading purple peas and pods. Marj knew their names: callistemon, acacia and hardenbergia. This country had to be something you sensed. How could she ever explain it? Of course Jimmy, if asked, would prefer the great, ordered English green, mazes of rose beds and interloping cream statues, but she didn't ask.

Rosy I'm strong, the letter continued, *like you've been. You stand so tall, I've learnt it from you. If you only flaunt your fear, it returns crumpled in your hand . . . and what's all this Molly thing? And who is this Marj person? You speak of her like family . . .*

Molly reread the last few sentences of the letter. Her mother was full of good sayings, words sounding profound and literate and important, but no one ever sure of their meaning. It baffled her. She thought of her mother—old and short and withered with piercing eyes that grabbed your attention, locking onlookers into her dreaming world, all head and no body. Marj was the opposite to Joyce

Moone, all body and fat, with a tidy open face. Yes, Molly did write of Marj as if she was one of the family. She felt caught out with her mother noticing.

sweet-smelling washing

IN TIME, Molly ventured outside the house by herself, beginning to relish the growing heat. She would sit out in the hot white sun long enough for her whole body to be heated through completely, as if in an oven, before retreating inside, into the womb of the house. There in the hall, sensing darkness on her face, she had to readjust her eyes.

Marj warned her not to step outdoors at midday, when the sun was at its full height. She told her she needed to protect her delicate skin. "You don't want blisters love," she shouted across the fence, "Your mother won't recognize you when she visits."

Marj Waters was teaching her neighbour everything. They met each other every day.

Each morning Molly would listen for the sloshing of water in the tub next door and the squeak of Marj's wringer. She waited for the flywire to shut with a bang, then followed her neighbour out into the day with her own laundry basket in front of her on the trolley laden with all kinds of wet washing.

Gone was the initial embarrassment over the choice of clothes to hang outside, and the possibility and need for privacy inside. Molly took her cue from Marj. She flaunted the clothes, whether they belonged to herself or to Jimmy, twirling the wet washing on the line defiantly, a daily gift to a sun god. She didn't even bother to hide the under-clothes by placing them in the middle of the line, on the shorter wires, shielded by bigger garments on the outside, but jumbled them up, copying Marj, and even handled Jimmy's underclothes with confidence.

"These are good drying days Molly," Marj's voice boomed, "Wet clothes all stiff and sweet-smelling by lunchtime." She stood in the middle of her garden, her large hands covering her thick hips, unafraid and laughing, her generous body vibrating. "Make sure you straighten the arms and collars, hems and pockets. Flatten them, shake them, crack and flick them, otherwise they stick. The sun makes them lie together, starched, all matted and as stiff as a board. Peel them apart love, and if you're careful, with your flicking and whipping, you don't need to iron much. The sun's a blessing and a curse; it dries and bakes you raw.

"There's nothing to fear though," Marj twirled, with her fat brown arms spread out in a dance, the washing swinging in time. She watched Molly struggle with the crosswires and pegs and height of the line. "The sky won't eat you love. Just treat it with respect!" And then as an afterthought she added: "One day you'll have a line full of nappies. White terry squares bleached and warm. Sweet for the little behinds. I've got dozens I can lend you when the time comes."

Molly reddened.

She was enjoying the warmth, not wanting to sacrifice it for anything. It was a sensation she looked for, hot and tingling all over, her eyes fully contracted and watery green, her body hair standing on end, she basked in it. She enjoyed gazing at the shimmer rising from the silver spiky leaves of the gums.

Marj said, "You haven't felt anything yet. Wait till it gets real hot, love. Then you'll be cooking!" Marj laughed at the migrant in a loose way, rattling her enormous chest. "You can't be in it for long! Ah no!"

December, 1960

Dear Mummy, Molly wrote, *I hang my washing out on the silver web, called a Hills hoist, and it dries in a morning to*

stiff paper. I don't iron here, only the special clothes, like Marj.
Did I tell you she's promised to take me up the mountain
behind the house? . . . And in answer to your hinting—yes,
Jimmy and I are fine, don't worry, I just don't talk about him
much, anyway, he's away at work all the time, busy, busy, busy
with soils. He's taking a while to settle in. His stuttering seems
to be getting worse I think. And no, I'm not having a child yet.
And no, I haven't got any work yet. Love Molly (that's what
Marj calls me—everything is shortened here and I like it).

At night Molly rocked herself to sleep thinking of Marj.
She was greedy for the likes of her neighbour's oven-baked
skin and as if to beckon that day closer, Molly repeated
some of Marj's words. Flatten them, shake them, crack and
flick them, she would say over and over again, otherwise
they stick. Peel them apart and flick them and whip them,
shake them and make them. Over and over and over again.
Bakes you raw, bakes you raw. The words became an
incantation to her, melodious music, a charm.

black gold

FOR A long time, Molly had only seen her neighbour out-side and always with the fence between them (apart from at the beginning when Marj had barged into the Browns' new house, unannounced). There was something protective about meeting each other around the washing line, con-versing over the fence. A confidence built up. And once the warm southern sky became an ally, once Molly had grown used to its perpetual yawn, anything was possible. The door to the Waters' house—the one Molly longed to go through —remained on the horizon, an entrance to a secret and private place. In time the gap between her green back door and the red one next door would narrow sufficiently for her to be invited in. Molly was sure. In the meantime, she learned to wait.

"Can you grow *anything*?" Marj did ask awkward ques-tions. "You know, in England, did you manage anything there?"

Molly was peering over the fence at Marj weeding the garden and pruning back the bushes from around the chicken pen.

"Geraniums. I had one in a pot once." Her young body pressed against the rough wooden fence.

"I see . . . oh well, you should manage something here."

Molly smiled. "Anything grows here."

"You're right love, we can grow the lot." Marj was away: "If you watch the rain and watering and frost and north winds and insects and bugs and have a good composted soil.

55

See, I can do it. Dig around, get rid of the weeds, water only when there's a dry spell, and love them. You've got to love plants to let them grow and flower. You've got to know inside you that it'll work." Marj looked triumphantly at her garden, then with slight impatience at her slowness. "I do the flowers in the church every week you see, so I have to have something flowering *every week*. Can't afford to miss a beat . . . They love me for it."

Marj folded her arms across her chest, fingers not quite reaching the opposite side. "I'll see you down there," she said, "If you're interested. It is after all the Church of *England*, you should be familiar with it. I'm only interested because of the flowers."

"Jimmy's not keen," Molly replied, "He doesn't believe really. In a good mood he calls himself an atheist. I'd like to go, it would remind me of home and Mummy, but I'll have to ask him."

"No you don't, no, no, no, he wouldn't know especially when he goes away on a trip which he's bound to do in this place. All the men go away at some stage. You don't have to ask him for permission."

"Uhm . . . well . . . I don't know, you see . . . I . . ."

"You mean you're afraid to cross him. My dear, let me tell you now, from one who's been married all these years— don't worry about it, but make sure you *do* it, that is—do your *own* thing. I do."

Marj threw her weight behind a garden fork. It sank into the soft ground.

"Oh by the way, I'll give you some cuttings, anything you need. It's a cinch. And I'll give you some compost, just like soil, if you turn it well the sour smell goes. Here, here's a bucketful. Feel it through your fingers and smell it!"

Molly did. She thrust her hand into the stuff and was surprised at how soft and moist it was. Black gold. At first it had a damp and lush smell, with a faint peppermint flavour. Burying deeper, she could smell the whiff of her home back in England, the pigeons in their cages and the mess she had to clear out in order to earn pocket money . . . shovelfuls of pigeon crap. Strangely, with the compost under her fingernails, she could smell her mother as well. Joyce was so closely aligned with her hobby, that the smell of pigeons never really escaped her body or clothes. Everything she touched had that faint and familiar aroma, although she had only Fudge left now. It was the same with her letters, even the paper Joyce wrote on. In the latest, the smell in keeping with the subject, she'd written, *Dear Rosy, I fly out at first light leaving the note scrawled in ink in my cage the feathers and fluff block out the sun until the pigeons fly high in a bunch around and up and down and around making patterns in the morning sky before meals are served. I love the ones that get lost the strays the runt finding it hard to catch up their wings having to work so hard. I fly out at first light . . . I would love some little ones soon don't be long with it. Don't you know I'm in hospital?*

Molly clasped the red bucket against her chest, full to the brim with Marj's compost. She tipped out the early Christmas present onto a turned bed. Upside down from out of the black moistness, handfuls of pink and brown worms crawled around, squirming and wriggling in knotted rings of soft flesh. As she watched the thick earthworms crawl about in her new soil, their movement made Molly think of Jimmy, his sands and loams and clays, and her mother's hopeless desires with the layette all ready; he was more interested in worms. Since being in Canberra they hadn't slept in the same bed; Jimmy would only touch her hand or sometimes lean into her shoulder, perhaps put an arm around her waist. On the ship it had been different, he'd wanted her close then. They'd slept on deck, side by side, holding hands. She should tell Marj about him sometime; they'd only seen each other at the beginning. It would form another link with her neighbour, although she'd be careful not to mention him too much. Jimmy would talk about earthworms at night over supper between mouthfuls, about all the millions burying into cool soil, in tight balls, curling to protect their moist bodies from dehydrating, from drying, from cracking and peeling. Then when the conditions were right, only then, they stretched out, grew fat by swallowing and discarding the soil they'd lived in as refuse. They moved tons of soil each day, he said. All over beneath the surface, dark loams and heavy red clays were on the move through the pink bodies of earthworms, Jimmy told her. He cradled worms in his large hand as he would a child.

Distracted but pleased with her efforts, Molly turned to give the bucket back to her neighbour. As she did so, the worms from the gift of compost disappeared quickly beneath the garden's surface. She'd wait now for the promise of flowers.

Marj called out, smiling at Molly's pleasure in digging, "Are you ready now? Will you come over and have a cup of tea? I think we need it. We could talk about the flowers you'd like."

This time Molly didn't refuse the offer. She knew it was to be the first of many. Shutting her own back door, she made her way down the garden to the gate at the back. She felt like a debutante being asked to dance for the very first time. And how different things looked from the other side of the fence. There was no going back.

calendar recipes

MARJ'S KITCHEN was the centre of the Waters' house, its shelves full of food in jars and canisters. It looked as if Marj lived in it. A table stood in the middle of the square room with enough space around it for her to fit sideways or squeeze past front on. A large armchair covered a frayed carpet square in one corner and there was a refrigerator in the other, above which were a collection of photos, family portraits of the children in sepia tones, their clothes and cheeks and lips touched up with watercolours in blues and reds and pinks. From the top of the Kelvinator, the family smiled—four boys and one girl, the baby.

"Here, run your finger around this flummery," Marj greeted Molly with food. "Tart! Isn't it? Lemons. I'll give you some if you like . . . if you like lemons that is. I use them in everything."

"I'd love some." Molly laughed with Marj, dipping her slim finger into the mixing bowl.

"Of course you would, I knew you would, especially after you taste this." Marj cracked another egg against the side of the bowl, opened the shell and lifted it high into the air shifting the yolk from one half shell to the other, letting the colourless glutinous insides drop with a splash into the middle of the frothy mixture. She saved the yellow yolk in a teacup. "We'll make you fat. Look at you, all skin and bones with no substance. We'll soon change that!"

"In summer when it's hot," Marj continued, the fat on her arm flapping in time with the flummery, "You know stinking, the thing to drink is lemon juice on ice. Made with freshly squeezed lemons, a peel or two, chopped mint from the garden and crushed ice. A must, after being out in the sun. I'll teach you all the tricks."

Transfixed, Molly watched Marj's fingers slip the yolks into the mixture so they broke and ran with the eggwhites to make it turn yellow. She folded and mixed with the spoons, then lifted the bowl to tip the light fluffy mixture into a serving dish. Dexterous. Sure. Light. Molly watched Marj with a kind of craving.

"Cooking with lemons is my speciality, you know," Marj was saying, putting a curl of candied peel into the centre of the dessert and sitting it in the refrigerator. "The kids got sick of them. Barbara can't eat them at all now, she was allergic after a time. I still cook them for myself though. Kevin loves everything I cook. It's the cooking that makes the difference, always, and how much sugar you use. But it's a good thing he's away at the moment. The strain is too much."

"Kevin?" At the mention of his name, Molly found she couldn't look at Marj: she had forgotten about Kevin, that one day he would return.

"Yeah, Kevin, the old man."

"He's not in the photos." Molly bent close to the row of five children, distracted and distant.

Marj licked her fingers and spoons clean and filled the kettle with water.

"No, I like that. Our photos aren't necessary, the old man's and mine. All grown up now they are."

"Do they live close by, the children?"

"Yeah, they're all here. We came here after we were married, with Tom on the way. In the very early days— pioneers really—when it wasn't much more than a thought on paper, like a construction site. Ah, we've watched it grow. Used to live down near Haig Park, in a farmhouse near the windbreak, but we've been in this house for a while now.

Ainslie is an old suburb, you can see by the garden I've got. All the new suburbs are treeless and lost at the end of bitumen roads. You're lucky to have moved in here really."

"Do you see them—the children?"

"Off and on. The four boys are married, their wives all get on. Tom's my eldest, then there's Frank, Richard and Rod. I've got ten grandchildren so far and I love them. I love spoiling them, much easier than your own."

"And Barbara?"

"Ah . . . she's always hoping to get married, but she never sticks to one person, pulls out at the last minute. She's had that many goes at it."

"She must be older than me."

"She is. The boys give her a hard time about it all."

"Have you got brothers or sisters?" Molly asked.

"No, I'm an only child. My mother was old when she had me."

"Me too. I suppose that's why I left."

"And your Dad?" Marj asked casually.

"War baby, I didn't know him. Mummy says he was nice, really nice. We lived with Grandpa mostly. He was like a father to me. Mummy said she loved having him in the house. When he died something happened, she changed, she began to sell off the pigeons." Molly's colour deepened, thinking she'd said too much, perhaps saying things out of turn. She'd never talked as openly to anyone before, Marj made it so natural. In the privacy of this kitchen she found herself talking about anything, her family, how she felt, the difficulties of getting work, that she did want to work. Later, it was Marj who suggested she look through the paper, with some success too. It wouldn't be long before she was about to start on a wedding in cream satin.

"We'll have good cup of tea now," Marj was saying, breaking up the conversation by filling the sink with dirty bowls. "I'll do this later, 'cause we've got to think more about your garden and what we can put in it," and then

61

she added, "There's a lemon tree down at the corner. A Sweet Rind. I used to get mine from there, now I've got my own. But it's tricky, put it in the wrong place and you've had it. One night will do enough damage. Not like up north—there they grow in any soil with no protection at all. Here, near the house is good. I learnt that after my first one died. Overnight it was, just like that, a really heavy frost I didn't know about till the morning, and then slowly over the next few weeks it went yellow then brown, from the top outside leaves to the trunk, its core. A slow horrible death. It was awful. I pulled it out and I cried, then planted another. We should get you one, from good rootstock. Put it in close to the house into the bed you're preparing. Facing north which is good, and it won't get the strong winds if we put it next to the steps."

"Do you think I can do it, grow something big?" Molly interrupted.

"Yes, of course, it'll start to flower and fruit with some love and care. Mark my words. Early next year, you'll have lemons too!" Marj's voice rose triumphantly. "You'll find they're useful for all sorts of reasons, and of course you'll grow things in your garden—just a little patience and time, the sun and soil does the rest."

Marj poured the tea into china cups and slumped into the comfortable chair.

"Here, I've got a cake too, something called a frangipanni cake with a macaroon topping—eggwhite and coconut. It's really a late January recipe, but I jump around the book, my Calendar of Cakes. The other one I use is the Calendar of Meats. Don't like keeping to the order they recommend —you know the CWA. It's a great book, I'll lend it to you sometime." Marj got up to unclasp the door to the meat safe. "I always keep them in here. This is from home. Mum didn't get to our wedding, but she gave me this safe, an original. I haven't done anything to it, except a bit of paint now and then. Kevin eats a lot of meat, so it's been handy as I used to keep it all in here before my Kelvinator arrived. Now I just use it for sweets . . ." She placed the cake in the middle of the table and cut it into six generous portions. "But tell me, when did you get married? You're still young like I was—just turned seventeen I was . . . It can't have been long ago."

"How do you know that?"

"I reckon you can tell. I've got you now." Marj waved her hand at Molly, and laughed till her flesh shook. "Well I'll tell you a secret—we've been gone thirty or more years, and I don't reckon it gets any easier or worse. The first twenty-four hours gives the whole game away . . . here, have another piece, it won't keep. In Australia you'll get fat. All this good food will make you fill out."

Together they ate cake and drained the pot of tea, and talked until late in the afternoon.

sun kiss

DEAR ROSY, Joyce had written,

   . . . Even in summer DO *wear clothes modestly. Don't forget my rule will you? One must never define one's private parts to the public with our clothes, wet or dry, hanging on the line or on our bodies, especially girls. Modesty is the rule. . . . Have you got any work yet?*

Every now and again ignoring her amnesia and obsession with pigeons, Joyce's eye would focus clearly and she'd pounce for the kill. At times like these she owned an eagle's eye. But she'd lost her authority with her daughter.

Discarding the letter, Molly fingered the shirring of her new fashionable bathers bought in Kingston on a shopping spree with Marj. She'd bought them spontaneously; Marj told her everyone swam in summer. They'd also been to a fabric shop and haberdashery.

Summer was a fine time for the body, and on a dreamy afternoon after lunch Molly was ready for some colour in her skin. The new bathers imitated her shape in parallel horizontal elastic lines, a bubbly curve down to her buttocks. Used to fitted suspender belts and circular-stitched bras, she felt naked and loose, but remained determined to change all of that as she straightened the bow between her breasts, looking for a cleavage, for fatness. She pressed both arms into her white bosom. Pouted her lips. Scanning herself in the full-length mirror, while bending one knee in mock modesty, she ignored the sight of her mother's letter caught in the reflection. As if in protest, she leant forward for a tube of lipstick on the dressing table. Cherry-Red, a colour Joyce loathed.

Outside, sheets of milky white clouds were pulled across a brilliant blue sky. It was irresistible from the back step. The sprinkler sprayed evenly across the hissing brown grass. It was cooler with it on, even though the water evaporated quickly into the hot still air. She watched rainbows come and go around the hemisphere of water as sunlight caught the droplets, painting their surfaces different colours. Cascading sprinkler prisms.

Within the privacy of her garden, Molly lay on her back under the clothes line and unclipped her straps. She shut her eyes to the cobalt glare, wrapped both arms around her head, listened to the flies and bees dipping into the brown grass of the hissing lawn and fell asleep.

The sun's warmth stroked her skin, senses dulled, from a grasping tingle to a slow burn.

"You'll turn into a chip!"

The voice startled Molly. It was late. Molly was stiff and warm.

Marj had walked into Molly's yard through the back gate, and was kneeling beside her, almost touching. "A water and lemon juice compress is what you need." Marj had a three-garden voice when she wanted. "You can't lie without cover. Not in this sun. It's like fire. You're scarlet!! Like a ripe tomato," she said, breathing heavily with a green frosted jug in hand.

From where Molly lay, Marj's wide brown kneecaps blocked the sun. The two had never been quite as close before, at least not in this way. Molly tilted her head for a sneak view of Marj's legs and a hidden triangular shape squashed between them at the top. Marj wore loose cotton panties at home, uninterested in controlling her figure with long bras and panty girdles. Fat and heat were her excuse.

"Naughty girl," Marj hummed to herself, pouring glasses

of lemon ice for them both. "Let *me* take care of you." The white triangle bulged.

Molly's straying eyes could see it was dark in there between the fat legs, shady and protected from the sun, cool. Marj's thick thighs lined the cavern generously.

"You English! You're a bunch of peeling watermelons! All the bloody same!"

Enthralled at being so close, Molly gazed at her neighbour's body, peeking at the impossible and private, conscious of Marj's ease, her chatter an agreeable camouflage. Even after such a short time of living next door, she felt close, poised for sharing deeper secrets, captivated by Marj's ability to be there, never enforcing or demanding. Marj didn't love or care to possess.

"What would Jimmy say?" Marj was saying, "I've got Kevin coming home next week and you've got your work to do. You'll have to smother your skin in oil you know. It'll peel off otherwise. The way you are love, it'll peel off for sure."

Molly's watery eyes ran over her friend's body again. She wanted to touch one of those fat brown knees. It was physically possible. So close. She could hold it tightly in her palm, her fingers pressing on the inside where the skin was lighter in shade, bone colour and baby soft. Failing that, she could lick the salty knee. Her lips were that close. Maybe it would be possible with an accidental brush, as she got up, coupled with thin apologies.

"Let's go inside," Marj said.

Molly drew breath.

"Come on. I'll help you up."

Molly clasped Marj's hand.

a gift of work

IN LONDON Molly's work had been everything. Each morning she would lay out the things she needed for the job: the wealthy client's specifications and measurements, the successful calico trial run, the standard pattern block she'd work off, the chosen materials in a roll, a box of pins, heavy sharpened scissors, a thimble, needles and threads, and her Singer machine with its converted electric power source that she had picked up in a pawn shop for a song. As she went to work her hands were dexterous, gifted. She knew exactly what to do at each stage, following the patterns and sequence of steps she'd devised in her head. She worked with authority and ease, willing the crepes and satins and lace and the finest of wools into shape with darts and tucks, gathers and pleats. Often, before the final fitting sessions, when she handed over the work wrapped in light tissue paper to the client, she'd try the garments on herself, dancing a polka around the room, encased in her own creation.

In Canberra, Molly had to be patient. It wasn't easy building up a clientele. With Marj's help she'd found a job already—a bride's dress in plain cream satin with a tulle veil, nothing fancy. And it was this she was thinking about, teasing out the pattern in her mind, when Marj popped in with an armful of flowers. Molly had been resting. Her skin was as rigid as an ironing board, on fire from the day before.

"Oh Marj, how lovely," Molly said, meeting Marj in the hall, barely able to move.

Marj shrugged her shoulders. "They were to be for the church, but I want you to have them." The flowers were from her garden, red bottlebrushes, wattles and native grasses. "You don't need plastic flowers here. Besides I want you to do something for me. You're very burnt, did you know that? What did Jimmy say?"

"What do you want me to do?" Molly said, choosing to ignore the questions. "And tell me what are these flowers?"

"That's a cedar wattle. This is a bottlebrush—callistemon. And kangaroo grass. And you wouldn't believe it, but they've got someone else doing the flowers this week, leftovers from a wedding on Saturday. I've *always* done St John's, even when there are weddings—they always ask me." Marj spoke with a flat voice.

"So what do you want me to do?"

"Barbara's getting married."

"Ah ha . . . at last. Do you think she'll go through with it this time?"

"She better. She says he's a reliable type and she's decided she wants to do the whole thing properly. I saw her this morning."

"You'll do the flowers?"

"Yes, and the food."

"And you want me to do the dresses of course."

"I told her all about you," Marj confessed, fingering the stems of the flowers now resting in Molly's arms. "She was very impressed. She'll tell her friends you're from London."

Hearing Marj say this made Molly smile. How exotic it sounded. What would they think if they had seen her at work at home? Joyce Moone let her use the lounge as a workroom although each evening before supper the table—the lot—had to be cleared. Molly would pack away the machine and its accessories and pick up the scraps and threads from off the carpet. Compared with everything else she had to share with her mother in that small house, the sewing table spread with folds of material and its upright wooden chair was a haven. With her back to the door and with her mind centred on the task ahead she could dissolve any frustration into her moving hands. It was hard work, for Joyce Moone hated being left out or ignored. She would hover in the shadows, interrupting at crucial moments with a string of mindless questions, just to get her daughter's attention. And when a client arrived to collect the finished garment, it was Joyce Moone who'd entertain and do all the talking. At times, you would have thought it was she who did all the work. Of course Molly knew how much Joyce loved the extra income, depended on it, and the clients paid well for the work was of the highest quality. Molly bought the sweet little extras of life, the things Joyce said she couldn't do without, the jewelled hatpin and cream kid gloves, the Victorian vase and the silver cutlery set.

"We'll pay of course," Marj was saying, "I'd love you to be part of it all. You have till Easter."

Molly hoped working in Australia would be different. To begin with, she had a room to herself and Jimmy let her leave the machine set up. She merely had to shut the door at the end of the day. She tried to understand his work too. He was finding it hard to settle; refusing to wear shorts, taking his cut lunch with him, rehearsing the things to say to his colleagues before he slept each night, poring over his textbooks. He'd stopped talking about it, preferring to dig in the back garden. There, he worked hard; it calmed him.

With her first job, the one she'd been thinking about, things were different too to what Molly expected. It was small and cheap. The bride thought a calico mock-up wasteful and unnecessary, happy to trust a good set of measurements: her eye for detailed perfection wasn't as seasoned as the London one. And then there was this opportunity, to work for Marj. Molly knew, even before she was told what Barbara wanted, that each tuck, every bead she sewed would be the best she'd ever done, a gift to Marj. All her London work had prepared her for this moment.

Molly hugged Marj. The armful of flowers lay pinned between them. "Of course I'll do it for you," she said, pressing her red skin against her neighbour's—it didn't matter that the hug hurt. "And thanks for the flowers."

"You need to put some sugar and bleach in the water and they should last a long time. I've got to fly."

They smiled at each other, letting go.

mountain gazing

IN THE cool of the afternoon, Marj led the way up Mount Ainslie. To get there, they went across the vacant block next to Molly's house and tramped through the bush until they came to a hole in a dilapidated wire fence. The discarded gate was padlocked and too high to climb, so Marj squeezed through the small opening, pressing her body against the wire. It was a close fit.

"Come on Molly, this is the way, that's it, through you go, I'll hold the top to make it easier, so you don't tear anything." For Molly, the hole in the fence was easy to get through, but Marj, ever thoughtful, made allowances for the newcomer where she didn't care so much for herself. Later, when she went up the mountain alone, Molly discovered there were ways around the hole, the disused fence being broken and lying on the ground further along. But something drove her to creep through the hole, even on her own. It was as if by squeezing through that hole at the foot of the mountain and remembering Marj's warmth, it entitled her to climb high enough to see the view.

The two women climbed, Marj going first to show the way, breathing hard, heavy footed. Fat in rings on her ankles. Molly watched the curve of Marj's dress and yellow housecoat ride up over the back of her wrinkled knees and dimpled thighs. In that housecoat, the one Marj used for dirty jobs such as washing up, raking out the chook pen and turning the compost, its front all soiled and marked, it was as if she'd walked from the back door into her garden, the mountain behind, as if she still thought she had privacy. Bare legs. No stockings or socks. What a contrast to Jimmy. Later, when Molly took him up the mountain he wore a suit, saying you never knew who you might meet, it could be important. He was restless and tore his scarf on the branch of a tree.

Molly and Marj climbed a gentle slope, dropped into a gully, before climbing up further onto the main scraggly ridge running from their two houses to the summit. They paused on a ledge, two-thirds of the way up, before the big push to the top.

The neighbours sat on a volcanic rock together to catch their breath and looked back over Canberra. Past the nestling houses and monuments, the view was good to the mountains beyond, the Brindabellas. They stretched along the horizon towards the south in a ribbon of purple and pink and blue, depending on the time of day. The capital lay at the mountain's feet, quite snug, between hills.

Marj pointed out all the landmarks of the town, her fat arm swaying, digging holes in the air. Parliament House, bleached white, St John's steeple, the War Memorial. The eagle with a huge wingspan perched on top of a tall pole, a gift from America. The flood plain and meandering willow trees of the Molonglo River over which the planned lake would wash. The old Commonwealth Avenue Bridge, and Kings Bridge under construction. She threw in the dome of the Science Academy, thinking Molly would be interested for Jimmy's sake. Everything was detached and separated by grassy expanses and paddocks and rows and circles of trees, so that from where Molly and Marj were perched, it looked as if you could pick up the pieces and rearrange the monuments and avenues, like a child's set of blocks.

However, it wasn't the monuments and landmarks that consumed Molly's interest. As Marj talked, Molly gazed at the high country, those spectacular humps lying in purple light along the horizon, rounded and tree-lined. The mountains lay quite still, like lounging naked women pleased with their shapes, their legs and arms and torsos and behinds all knotted in an early evening haze. She imagined all the tiny life of birds and flowers and insects and butterflies crawling over their fleshy sides. It gave her goose pimples, similar to when she first met Marj. She would discover early morning and late afternoon were the best times to view the Brindabellas. And one day Molly hoped to climb her favourite—Tidbinbilla Peak—the pimple in the middle.

Their bottoms grew cold and numb from the hard flat rock.

"Come on, the last push. Up we go!" Marj encouraged herself more than Molly. Marj was exhausted but determined.

Step by step and with flies on their backs, they scrambled up the final lip. Molly followed the swaying skirt and ankles, till the two women stood triumphantly on either side of a survey peg, with their legs apart and hands on hips. Open smiles through heavy breathing.

"Molly . . . you'd think I was born here with all my talk. Wouldn't you? You can talk about this place forever and each time I add a bit I feel it's more and more mine."

Molly's words in reply were beginning to form, tickling the back of her throat, but her mouth was dry. She could see the mountains clearly now, her women in their Turkish bath, unashamed of their colour and nakedness and position, lying low in the steamy haze.

"I love this town." Marj penetrated her thoughts.

Molly wanted to say something in return but the climb had covered her with a thin gauze of silence, too precious to tear. And her mind began to wander, wondering about Jimmy digging holes in the ground down there at her feet, wondering whether he felt the same way in his search for sounds as she did now. Did he brush against the folds of the gauze which covered him in his struggle for a voice? Touch its creases with his lips as the words tickled *his* throat? Was it feasting—as it was for her now? Or fear of never being able to form the words that held him back? Feasting or fear?

In her gut and by the look he would get on his face, Molly knew it was the latter. Her husband did most things out of a well of fear, she was beginning to see. Every spare moment at home now was spent digging a pit in the garden. It was two yards long and deepening. She could watch him from the kitchen window. Was Marj aware of the hole? He'd learn more about the local soils this way, he argued, away from critical eyes, in private, without having to talk. With his face contorted and an oily string of hair across his eyes, he dug with a sharp pointed spade. By slicing the dense clay down the face of the blade he could carve out a smooth cross-section of the profile, like a clean slice of heavy Christmas cake.

But with Marj beside her it didn't matter for the moment, and Jimmy was a long way off down the hill. With a corner of a smile, Molly feasted on her thoughts, knowing these thoughts were as important as the mountains lying there, within reach.

"My heart, of course," Marj was saying, "is up north, in Queensland with the pineapples and avocado pears where I grew up. But when you've lived in a place for as long as I have and brought up all your children as well, it kind of grows on you. You become part of the design. You'll have to watch it Molly. Before you know what will happen, you'll be part of the plan too!"

Molly laughed with release.

"You'll have to get your name on the bottom of the lake. I've arranged to do it with a cold chisel, on a pylon of the big bridge when it gets started, right at the bottom. Or you could do it on the retaining wall when it gets built, in the wet concrete. It'll be there forever then, a monument for the future all covered with murky water. You should do the same as me, while the topsoil is being dug out for all the gardens and parks, before the bed is filled up. Jimmy doesn't have to know!"

They grinned.

"Come on Molly," Marj wiped her sweaty temples with a finger, "Let's go, it's late and I'm hungry. We'll roll down the hill to tea."

see-through blue eyes

"HEY, COME and join us." Marj called out across the fence with a tempered voice.

Sunday. The air was dreamy. Soft and blue and careless.

"Jimmy . . . Molly . . . come and meet Kevin. He's back. And I've got Barb's measurements for you Molly."

On the other side of the paling fence and close to the bird-bath, a huge man lounged in a fold-out canvas chair, the lapping seat inches from the freshly mown lawn. Barefoot and in a blue singlet and shorts, the man drank beer.

"*This* is Kevin," Marj flung an arm in the man's direction, proudly. "Off work for a couple of weeks! Over Christmas."

Kevin Waters *was* fat. The fat didn't encircle his body in a neat parcel, but swam around his bones, in colossal and sustained horizontal and vertical waves, a carnival of excess, glistening brown with sweat. Kevin's arm was bigger than Molly's thigh, and even the front of his calves seemed to wobble.

"Come on Molly, bring Jimmy, you all need to meet one another. It's been too long already." Marj laughed carelessly.

Molly sat, settled in a canvas chair, with her green sunglasses and a straw sunhat down over her ears. Opposite Kevin. She felt the warmth of the sun seeping through her loose cotton blouse.

Jimmy sat beside Molly in an upright chair making him seem taller than ever. He was all in white, with sandals. Straight-backed, stiff, silent.

"Here, have a drink. Jim, it is Jim, a beer?"

76

Jimmy licked his separated teeth. Stretched his lips.

Molly answered for him, "Thanks, thanks a lot. Yes, it's Jim, that's right."

Kevin gestured to her questioningly, a beer in his hand.

"Oh yes, thank you, yes, I'll have a drink."

"Love, get us a glass will you," Kevin motioned to Marj.

Molly held a tall cold glass of frothing beer in her hand like Marj, and drank small sips from time to time. Cool to her lips. Jimmy was too tongue-tied to drink. His grip around his glass was tight, the other hand nailed to his knee, knuckles white.

Kevin turned to face Jimmy, pushing up the edge of his hat so it sat back on his head.

"You'll have to get onto that lawn you know. It'll get away from you."

"Oh yes, it gr–gr–ggggrows qu–qu–quick . . . f–f–ast." Jimmy groped for words, any word, his throat and Adam's apple vibrating madly, raw with the strain. His face was scarlet.

Kevin's eyes dilated. Eyebrows raised.

"You know there are snakes," Kevin faced Molly this time. "They come down from the mountain. You've got to tread carefully."

"Kev stop it will you."

"No, I'm only warning them, you've got to be careful. Venomous snakes and spiders are a real part of Australia."

"Along with flies and maggots and weevils . . . the list goes on." Molly piped in, surprised at her own voice.

"Would you like something more to eat?" Marj asked, breaking up the conversation into crumbs. "A piece of pie, or a scone, or a meringue? Jimmy? You look like you need it." She passed the plates around in circles and figures of eight. Once started, Jimmy ate continuously, jabbing the sweet food with a silver-plated cake fork. He tried everything on the table. He felt safer with food in his mouth.

"So you like rocks and, er, what was it, dirt?" Kevin asked.

"Er, not d—dddddirt, b—but s—s—soil." Jimmy couldn't help the correction even with his mouth full of whipped cream.

"Soil then, you're a scientist, uh. Well, well. I can see you've got a thing about it. That hole looks like it's coming on. You'll get to the bottom of it soon. Just don't fall in! Down to earth. Dust to dust." Kevin laughed at his own joke, his throat shuddering like rippling jelly. "Look, sorry mate," he raised his glass wildly, "I don't mind a bit of earth myself under the nails, but I couldn't sit in it all day. I reckon I'd go mad thinking of what's buried there."

"Kevin! Not everywhere." Marj tried to defend Jimmy while passing another meringue. "It has other uses than that. Jimmy's learning. I think his digging is good. He's doing important work."

"What would the Poms know about it anyway? I reckon I know more digging roads with my jackhammer." Kevin's top lip was wet with sweat.

"If it wasn't for soil, Kevin," Marj said, "I wouldn't have a garden. Anyway, did you know Molly has agreed to do Barb's dress and the other girls' too? She's good with her hands. We'll get a photo in *The Canberra Times* I reckon, if Barb agrees to St John's. They always do them there. The grounds are beautiful."

Kevin was silent, gulping his drink. When he relaxed, his face was kindly, Molly thought, there was a trace of the younger man in him. She thought she could see what drew Marj to him.

"Here are the measurements." Marj handed her friend a page of detailed cross-references. Bust, waist, hips, neck, wrist, neck to knee, armpit to wrist. Waist to ankle.

After tea, the four neighbours continued to sit in the outdoor canvas furniture, waiting for a coming summer storm, for the first drop of rain to hit the water lying in the bird-bath. On the picnic table, half-eaten lemon pies and biscuit-sized meringues squashed together with generous helpings of cream lay spread out. There was a fly swat and Marj's centre-piece too.

The sky darkened. The air was dense and in the distance lightning glittered in flickering tongues. For something to do, Kevin fingered a scarlet gladiolus askew in Marj's bouquet, his arm flat across the damask. Only the tips of his fingers moved. He fiddled with the frill at the edge, teasing it, playing with it, while the others watched in awkward silence, and then pushed his forefinger into the funnel until it was full to bursting. Aware of Molly's curious eyes, he swore under his breath as the head tore, and took the whole flower out of the cut glass vase, spraying water and gluey sap from its stem. He pulled it apart, his blue eyes cloudy, yellow pollen dazzling his finger.

"Oh Kevin!" Marj moaned, as to a child, then whispered into Molly's ear, "He loves them really."

"Sorry Marj . . . I'll pick a new one . . ."

It was time to go, Molly decided. She was watching Marj rake the torn scarlet fragments into a pile. "Jimmy . . ." she said. To hide his face, Jimmy was folding the ribbed edge of his sock over the white elastic garters with absolute precision. "Let's go home . . . before the rain."

sculptured bodies

"WE NEED to t–t–talk, ttttalk," Jimmy insisted, pulling Molly from the back door through the house to the front porch. The fly door banged against the door frame. "We'll t–t–t–talk, we'll talk here, where they ccccccc–can't hear us." His huge hand enveloped hers.

"What about?" she asked, "What do you want to talk about?"

"Them. I don't l–like them. There's s–s–something smelly . . . f–ffffishy–." Jimmy was losing momentum, whistling between difficult words.

Molly let go of his hand and grasped the pole on the porch instead.

"Marj is all right, you can't say anything against her."

"Yes, I know, M–MMMM–, you s–s–sssee more of M–M–Marj than you do m–me."

"You're always working. She's teaching me everything. I like Marj. This place wouldn't be the same without her."

Jimmy was silent. He rocked backwards and forwards.

"In fact you go away . . . when . . .?" she asked.

"Soon. It's a bbb–bb–bbig one, way n–n–north," he said. A pinhole stream of air escaped him in a sigh.

"Okay, soon—so you say I can't talk to anyone! What am I to do then? I need to meet people, Jimmy." She raised her voice. "You've got your work you know and now I'm busy with mine."

"Sshh . . . Marj, yes, but not K–K–K, you know K–K–." His eyes rolled white as he groped for the word.

"Kevin. He's all right. He belongs to Marj. Two halves of each other, she knows what she's doing."

"He m–makes me f–ffff–, he mmmmakes me fff–feel uncccc–comfortable."

"Oh that's rubbish, he was just having a go at you in jest. He didn't mean it, they've been together for years, it's just that we haven't met him before. He's all right. I'm sure we'll get to like him like everything else here. You're making a great hole too, learning a lot, and besides he's probably jealous. You, you've just got to flaunt yourself, like Marj does." Molly began to talk as confidently as her friend, with a strong voice. "Do you see how she does it with *her* size? Just let it speak, spread the jam thickly, that's the way to do it. You've got nothing to be ashamed of. Hold your head high . . ."

"D–don't l–l–leave me," he interrupted, swinging around to face Molly, "Please."

He clasped her and she felt his warm arms keenly, as if after a very hot day of drying out in the sun she sipped water from a tumbler, but only enough to wet her lips. She craved more. She wanted Jimmy to hold her, press into her side, engulf her with his whole body. She wanted to feel him like never before for at last he was touching her. She wanted to feel *somebody*—another human.

"Cccc–ccan you h–h–h–," the sounds he made dug into her face as keenly as a pick into sandstone, "H–h–hold me ttttt–ttt–." Jimmy's fingers tightened, his grip burning her skin. "Tonight?" He stood back. The rock he was on splintered.

Can you hold me tonight, he'd asked.

Oh God, she whispered.

Molly thought about the double sheets given by her mother at their wedding. They were the best, a gift-set of two sheets and four pillowcases folded into a smooth glossy box with gold writing, and wrapped with a white ribbon. Tight clear-view plastic across the top allowed you inspect the neat package. Molly had left them boxed in for weeks at the bottom of a trunk. The double bed lay empty. Then, as she grew accustomed to washing with Marj in the morning, the two women being party to each other's laundry, she tore the cellophane top and threw them all into the machine, recklessly, feeding the Whirlpool lies of a happy conjugal bed. From then on, Molly washed them every two weeks without guilt, and folded the dry sheets into a flat bundle to fit back into the white box tied with the satin ribbon.

"Yes, I'll do it, I'll make up the big bed with Mummy's sheets."

Much later, Molly lay motionless between the white cotton sheets, quite bare. Jimmy lay close to her in a parallel line down the bed, his feet over the end of the mattress. He wore a singlet and oversized white elasticized shorts so that she felt his warmth but not his skin. Molly traced patterns in the ceiling with her eyes, rectangles and triangles, thinking about the afternoon, about Marj and Kevin and their fat bodies, wondering how they slept, how they fitted in a double bed. She gazed at the light fittings above her, shaped like a girl's breasts with brass knobs at the tips. Jimmy lay still, quite still, on edge. If only he would thrust out a long arm, touch her bare skin.

She remembered sleeping together on the ship's deck, fully clothed; how they held hands almost recklessly, thrilled with cheekiness and touch. Close to the equator and as the nights had grown warmer, the deck was preferable to the stale airless cabins, those sultry overcrowded ovens. Although it had taken a week of sleeping in sweat to bring the honeymoon couple to the deck, once there, the two lay on the ship's grey blankets, side by side, holding hands in the dark. A gentle night breeze from the ship's movement kept them cool and they managed to get some sleep.

Canberra had broken the romantic hand-holding spell, something pushed Jimmy away, he wouldn't come close.

Molly didn't understand, but couldn't find the words to ask about it. Without discussion, he'd chosen the smallest room, sleeping all curled up on a camp bed, with a square table for his work and books. Molly had the middle room for her sewing, and slept in the main bedroom. The double bed with its carved wooden ends and a covering of red satin dominated this room, but she couldn't sleep on it. For there on her own, thinking of Jimmy and crying herself to sleep, Molly was lost at sea, in deep water and unable to touch the sandy bottom. She would spend the night struggling to keep her head above the white froth, rising and falling helplessly with the waves of the double mattress. After a week of sleepless nights, she tossed dirty clothes on it and chose a wrought iron single bed instead, sleeping between tightly tucked-in sheets. Pushed under the windowsill, it was meant for visitors. From the comfort of her pillow, she was able to see a slice of the sky clearly, for nothing blocked her view. She watched the phases of the moon, crowds of stars gathering in the darkness to form the Milky Way, and the morning sun break up the dancing party. If she lay there during the day, she became lost in the weightless blue air, watching rosellas and parrots and cockatoos exercise in swooping circles, looking for animal shapes in the clouds.

Jimmy's fingers twitched. She waited, longing for him to touch her.

"Rosy, you, you awake?"

There was a crackle in his voice.

"Yes, I am." Yes, she was awake, of course she was awake. She felt her shape in the bed as if sculptured out of wet sand, each curve and bend pressing against the bottom sheet. Did Marj wait with Kevin? *Wilt thou have this Man to thy wedded husband? Wilt thou obey him, and serve him, love, honour and keep him in sickness and in health? Wilt thou wait for him? By him? With him? Wilt thou wait ON him? So long as ye both shall live?*

"I ccc–an have a d–d–day off," Jimmy continued. "A

l–l–ong weekend before I ggg–gggg–go away." He breathed deeply as she waited for more.

"What, a holiday?"

"Yes."

"So soon?"

"Because I'm g–going away."

"Oh," she replied.

Jimmy crinkled his forehead, curled his body a little to fit into the bed, and squeezed his toes down into the crack at the end of the bed. Molly sensed his unease. She knew his job was tough—though he refused to talk about it unless pressed—home late, working at weekends, the field trips. Up until now it had been day excursions in and out of Canberra, but his name was down for the first surveying trip of the year, up north. His superiors thought he should go; they wanted to see him perform. That meant sleeping out in tents and having to mix closely with others. In jest, his colleagues began to prepare Jimmy with stories of giant mosquitoes, and of goannas climbing up the bodies of newcomers. These prehistoric creatures could smell the difference, they said.

Jimmy's salvation for the moment was his digging at home. It calmed him. From the kitchen window Molly would watch him. The mound of dug-up red and mottled clay around the edge of the pit grew large and round, and it didn't take long before he disappeared down the hole altogether, his head bobbing up and down with the work. And every time he dug, Jimmy fiddled with bottles, solutions and charts. He described and tested each layer of soil again and again, filling out sheets of paper with elaborate codes as he would do in the field, under the heading, AINSLIE SOIL BY DR JAMES BROWN. He learned to roll a good bolus in the Australian way. With a clod in his hand, he kneaded the earth into a ball as you would a knob of pastry. Then, using his two hands as a rolling pin, he fashioned them into long rods, in order to make rings and bracelets. He'd hold them up for Molly to see. If there was a high percentage of clay, the rods circled without cracking. He practised fastidiously —the pH, colour, texture, soluble salts and structure—as if there had to be some slight variation in the soils from day to day or week to week, essential for him to pick up and record. A bottle of clean water and a small square towel sat on the edge of the pit for when he finished. Molly would watch him cleaning up, a master of the art, wondering why he'd chosen this job, and why he worked himself so hard.

And now he was contemplating a field trip, a big one as he said, that would take him out of Canberra. And Molly knew without his saying that the biggest hurdle would be the presence of the other scientists. Jimmy wouldn't be alone; they'd do things differently. The Englishman's field skills were to be put to the test.

"How long are you away for?" she asked.

"Eight www–wwweeks."

Molly's mind reeled with the possibilities. "Eight weeks!" A lot can happen in that sort of time, she was thinking.

"We'll go in the cccc–car."

"What? Where?"

"On our h–h–holiday, out of C–C–Canberra."

"Oh us?" The idea of a trip with Jimmy, just then, was furthest from her thoughts. "To the mountains then."

"Too rough."

"To Sydney?"

"No. No." Jimmy hammered the word. He hated big cities and that was one of the reasons he had left London.

"To the beach then." Molly was emphatic.

Ah, the beach. Yes, she had to go to the beach, it was obvious, to that strip of sand all around the wide-bodied continent. Troubles leave you at the beach, the baking sun gives you a thickened leathery skin. The beach was what had attracted Molly from afar. The rolling, dumping surf and miles and miles of white white sand. Besides, she'd heard so much about the coastline from her friend. Marj knew how to drive, and had promised to take Molly in her Vanguard to the south coast—Bateman's Bay, Pretty Beach and Bawley Point, and also up north, across the border to Queensland's beaches, her home territory.

"Jimmy, we'll go to the beach," Molly said with a firm voice.

She would have to work hard on this suggestion, for if they talked about the trip too much, he'd back off, and she'd relent, knowing it was unfair. But Molly was determined to get her own way, more than ever.

Jimmy was silent. The bed creaked.

She relied on Jimmy driving their new car, not having a licence herself. She could see their new two-tone Holden at the water's edge, but found it hard to imagine *him* lounging on the bonnet, for she knew Jimmy hated the water, unequivocally. He had first revealed this to her in the early days, as they walked the streets of London together, separate, not touching, but their feet in rhythmic step. Was it a caution? And then on the ship, he told her about his mother, Mrs Ethel Brown, the very beautiful widow. The young boy would lie awake at night, listening to the dull thud of footsteps on the stairs, the squeak of an unoiled door being shut, a muttered curse at the noise, and then her laughter. It was his mother's laughter that he waited for, blinking wildly to keep his eyes open and free from sleep, rubbing them with his small fists. He adored her when she laughed. Some nights he would have to wait up so long, never sure that he had heard the trill of her laughter, for it could have been more in his dreaming world; but on others, there was no mistake. Ethel laughed like no one else. It came from deep within, in rippling arpeggios of ecstasy, quite infectious, so that the young boy found himself grinning with pleasure, his hands smothering his mouth with the sheet. He let out little chuckles and guffaws. He was ready to burst.

But he could never precipitate her laughter himself. He tried, oh how hard he tried, laughing himself, telling her jokes, rather wet ones he had to say, and tickling her in the soft places, those places that made his fingers fairly tingle with pleasure and envy. To no avail. He had to accept the unexpectedness of her laughter, and learn to lie awake at night listening for the dull thud thud up the stairwell and accompanying cascade of mirth, so that when it came, when she laughed like water suddenly pouring down a drought-stricken rock face, sweetly fresh, he would hold his breath, not daring to breathe, conscious then of the way a whirling happiness came at him minced with pain.

A quick-witted passer-by had tried to resuscitate her. That's what all the papers agreed on the morning after. They had a picture of the saintly man from behind, a man in a brown mac belted in tightly at the waist and the mac wet like his trousers, his face covered completely by an elegant Trilby hat. The newspapers, in the nasty narrow columns devoted salaciously to the case, made the unforgivable suggestion that Mrs Brown knew the man in the brown mac and Trilby hat. No, they went further it would seem if you were to read the small print, and this Jimmy did, over and over. He glued the articles carefully, piece by piece, between the thick cardboard covers of an exercise book now yellow with age and torn at the edges. It went with him everywhere.

"Marj says there's a beach that's easy to get to, that's close . . . and safe," Molly said. "Good for a weekend trip I'm sure. It'll be wonderful. And I'd love to learn how to swim here." She touched the pearls around her neck, the two pearl eggs on each ear she wore everywhere.

"On one c–cond–dition." It was as if Jimmy would do anything for Molly.

"What's that?"

"I don't have t–to g–go in."

"Done. Of course, all I can do is paddle you know.

"It's going to rain now Jimmy, a summer storm."

Molly loved the flash of lightning, party lights in the

sky, counting the miles as Marj taught her, and waiting for the rumble of thunder, especially now, as a distraction. She remembered sitting in Marj's garden in the low canvas chairs, watching the afternoon storm brew.

"I like the rain. The ocean turned upside down."

And then, without any warning, Jimmy reached over and pulled Molly's head towards his own. His movement startled Molly. He held her for a time in his big hands, watching her eyes. Molly wondered if Jimmy read her mind, if he liked what he saw, or was he too caught up with his memories. When the man in the brown mac found her, a thick seaweed of blood and glass beads swam around her body and neck. The hat she had been chasing was her favourite too—Jimmy had known Molly would like that detail—made of stiff linen, with pretty imitation flowers on one side.

She felt his big hands covering her warm face, when suddenly, he bent over her and kissed her cheek, kissed it hard, sweetly at first, open-mouthed, then a bite with blood. An electric shot exploded through her body as his tongue explored her skin. Molly reeled back, frightened by his strength and her desire.

"I'm s–s–s–sorry RRRRoses, it was too, too s–s–ssssoft. So soft. Irresi–irresi– . . . Didn't mean to hurt you." He mouthed the last sentence, touching her shoulder gently.

Molly heard the patter of light rain, softly at first, then harder and louder, banging a song on their red roof. She turned away and listened to the notes, to the lyrical cry sweeping over their house, the heaven-sent rainwater waves of sound. She wanted to feel him more than anything, touch his lips with hers, fold their bodies together into one, but felt distracted. Her mind was skipping from flower to flower like a butterfly looking for nectar, thinking now of her neighbours, wondering if Kevin bit Marj as Jimmy had kissed her. She put her hand up to her cheek and smeared the blood over her pale skin while treacle rain, the colour of night, splashed and slid against the half closed window.

"Rosy, I'm s—sorry."

"It hurt," she said smudging the circle with tears, trying to rub it out.

"I won't t—t—touch you again like—like that," Jimmy offered.

"It'll bruise Jimmy," she said getting her strength back. "It'll show. I'll see Marj tomorrow. She'll guess. She'll tell me it's you: It's Jim, it's that Jimmy, isn't it? she'll say. She'll know straight away, and I won't have to say anything, I'll stand there knowing I can't hide it, knowing I don't want to hide it." Molly blushed and her lips fluttered a little although Jimmy didn't notice, cowering on the bed, all strung up in the bedding.

"Rosy I said . . ."

She watched the treacle splash and bounce and slide while dabbing her cheek with a corner of the white sheet.

"We can st—ssst—st—ill lie in the sssss—same bed t—t—tonight," he added. Yes, please, she wanted to say, but didn't say a word.

They did lie beside each other that night, her cheek red from the bite, and his craving but impotent body turned in a curve to the outside, the hollow interior warm and small and protected. She wanted to reach out, to touch him, to rest her hot fingers on the skin of his back, but found she couldn't. Her body had a drowning weight to it that night.

The next morning it was still raining, intermittently, with a light patter against the glass. After Jimmy got up, she slipped into the pocket of her own bed underneath the open window. And in her slice of sky she saw a rainbow remnant, rings of pale colour in a pool of early morning light: concentrated at one end, faint and sanded back at the other. While Jimmy began the day by shaving with a pot of cream in the bathroom, Molly danced a slow waltz with the coloured ribbon. The rainbow had completely disappeared by the time he said goodbye.

Molly bought a jar of rainbow balls from the grocery store in the Civic Centre. She sucked on the striped boiled lollies after lunch as a treat, while she cut out the cream Chantilly lace sleeves of Barbara's bridal gown with sharp scissors.

Later, she wrote to Joyce:

end of December

Dear Mummy,

We're really busy here now. It's Christmas, but you wouldn't know—it doesn't seem right somehow in the heat, just more food on Marj's table! At least Jimmy is occupied going to his office and digging at home, while Marj's Kevin sleeps, except when she feeds him. You can smell him in their house. He agitates Jimmy so much so he can't say his name any more. His k's are terrible. But it should be all right because Jimmy's got a small holiday, a long weekend, and I'm trying to persuade him to go to the beach, before he goes for months. I'll be fully occupied with Barbara's wedding coming up. I think all their savings will be poured into it, she's their only daughter. I'm doing all of the dresses:

the bridal gown (Chantilly lace gown, tulle veil encrusted with beads)

three bridesmaids (full-length silk organza dresses in shades of green and lemon with feathered white curvettes for their heads)

a flower girl (in apricot silk and a circlet of flowers over her curls)

Marj gets very excited about it all, and can't believe her luck at having me next door. She'll be doing all the catering, and what a spread it will be—she's putting away bits and pieces already, all her favourite recipes. We'll be eating the leftovers forever!

custard cream puffs and wedding clothes

IT WAS clear Kevin drank heavily, his beer like water. Marj unloaded cases of bottles every few days. She loved pampering him, feeding him with the best of her cooking, using a calendar book for ideas. When he was asleep in the afternoon, Molly would go over and help her, or just sit and watch with some hand sewing and a cup of tea. They could hear him snoring in the bedroom.

Marj said, "You'll get used to him soon enough."

Marj gave Molly the easy jobs to do—reading the recipe out loud, or mixing the dry ingredients, beating the eggs or even sometimes smoothing the translucent icing onto a cake. They made Chicken Charlotte and custard cream puffs, steak and kidney pie and rice pudding. Marj said by helping there was a bit of them both in every dish—savoury and sweet. On these days Molly took half home for tea: Jimmy preferred this arrangement, thinking it was better than cheese on toast under the grill.

"It's a real communion," Marj said, "Even though we eat the food with our own husbands in separate houses."

They went to church with each other too, off and on, and knelt very close at the altar rail, their arms nearly touching. While back in their homes they'd gouge out the warm doughy centre of a loaf, at church, they swallowed a small cube of bread flattened by the clergyman's fingers.

Kevin never went with them. He would stay at home surrounded by empty bottles.

Molly watched him from a distance, cautiously. She liked his milky see-through eyes, but was repulsed by his fatty smell: a sweet manly smell mixed with raw sweat, a cocktail spread over hair and skin. It made her nauseous. She understood why Marj kept so many bars of soap in her bathroom, a collection of perfumed flowers and fruits of different sizes piled high in glass canisters on the window ledge—Mandarin, Lavender and Green Apple—and eucalyptus oil in purple bottles. And above the vanity basin and mirror decorated with frosted ducks and glass knobs, there was an old biscuit tin with yellow wattle on its lid. Inside was a collection of pink crystals and white balls as hard as hail. Marj said bath salts stopped headaches.

"Oil and smelly soap, my dear, Secret Weapons, I enjoy pampering myself, I do. The salts help to perfume and soften the water. He's a teddy bear really—harmless, big body, small muscle. He's always been a softy inside—that's why I married him. You just have to let them get on with it—lie low is my motto. You can always clean up the mess in the end when he falls asleep. It's quick you know." It was as if Marj knew Molly needed all the help she could give. The bite on her cheek was still clear; a scab now, in the shape of a set of teeth.

Molly remembered seeing Marj's bathroom for the first time—a larger version of her own in different colours—and twirling in the centre with bare open arms, pretending she was a dancer, with Marj laughing and squeezing her tight (she was used to hugging her friend by now). Like a child, she whizzed around, carelessly opening all the pots and bottles and little drawers full of secret things for women only. And she peered through the slatted louvres, wondering whether at night she would be able to see a sequined sky and so muster the stars' applause.

"Sure, have a whiff," Marj said. "I've had these for a long time. They make any skin soft like dough. A smell of the bush. I'll give you a bath one day and show you." Molly listened to the trickle of Marj's laughter. "But don't tell the old man, you can't tell him anything until it's certain, like the wedding for instance. He hates any make-up or cosmetic or artificial extra. He hates fuss. These are special though. My skin is so shocking, so dry and lumpy in this climate. Made from the natural oil in the eucalyptus leaves. You'll feel like a baby all over again."

Molly knew now who Marj referred to, the *old man*, fatter than anybody, with see-through button blue eyes. Sometimes Marj called him Dad: she was a little girl with Kevin home, and Molly decided she was going to like him.

The day before Molly and Jimmy left for the south coast, the two women pored over the pieces of cut-out material and the calico trials on the floor in Molly's sewing room. The wedding party, and all its finery, was beginning to take shape in Molly's mind.

"Have I made it too big?" Molly asked.

"She's a big girl Molly. Like me," Marj answered.

"Now we have to think of you Marj. You've got to look good too, you know—get you out of those sacks and house-coats for a day!"

Marj ran both her hands around her waist and hips, eyes puckered, "Not grey please, like a funeral."

"No . . . I think a greenish colour. I've got a piece in my trunk. I was going to make it up for myself . . ."

"It's got to be right Molly. Barb's particular."

"So am I," Molly said disappearing into her room. She came back dragging a length of fine linen in a deep olive green and put it up to Marj's generous body, draping it around in an arc to the back while she stood at arm's length.

"Perfect. You'll be the best dressed there! I'll think about the pattern while I'm away."

Marj said, "Get into the water won't you, get wet, I do every time. I'd love to be coming with you."

"I know."

The next morning Marj saw Jimmy and Molly off early with a wave and a hamper of food for their trip.

bottled oceans

JIMMY DROVE haphazardly, jerking the pedals with his large clumsy feet, first the clutch then the accelerator and finally the brake, paralysed by the open road, the speedometer and passing cars, not used to driving long distances. They were on their way to the coast across the southern tablelands and over Clyde Mountain, along a road that swung recklessly between bitumen and dirt surfaces. Overtaking was a nightmare. On the bitumen sections, he tried to swing the maroon and cream Holden into the oncoming traffic, but lost courage at the last moment, braking wildly, afraid of the speeding trees and gravel edges. Like a bad smell, he hung behind lorries and laden trucks. It was after a scare on their way that he told Molly he'd leave the driving to others on the field trip up north.

This was the Browns' first trip out of Canberra in their brand-new Holden. They'd bought the car from a dealer who in a kindly way didn't comment on how the English couple jerked out of the car yard on a test-drive, shrouded in clouds of dust. Molly had stared straight ahead, pulling her hat further down over her ears while pouting her made-up red lips.

It wasn't long before they had to leave the transparent open spaces of the tableland country at the top of Clyde Mountain. They went over a lip at the edge and so down, down, down into the valley below. The ground seemed to drop away into space, opening up a narrow crack on the escarpment's steep side just wide enough for a car to squeeze through. The change in landform was both abrupt and startling: they were unprepared.

In other circumstances her first taste of rainforest should have arrested Molly's attention, the way the light snatched its breath as the vegetation grew bigger, thicker, taller, the way it trickled down through whatever space it could find, filtering through the fat transpiring leaves of the canopy by stealth. But the descent down the escarpment was narrow and steep, a series of hairpin bends, quite treacherous in places. Cars hooted and honked, their drivers waving angry fists at Jimmy who smothered the wheel and filled the front bench seat and half the windscreen, his jaw locked. There was no room for turning back. Molly hung onto the armrest, her knuckles white, and tried to think about other things; for a start, there was another letter from her mother she'd tucked under Marj's hamper on the back seat. She'd opened it the day before and it worried her, her mother was sick.

They reached the bottom in silence. The road flattened. Refusing to navigate the punt across the river at Bateman's Bay, Jimmy turned left at the intersection and headed north for Bawley Point.

Molly had almost given up hope of seeing the ocean as they crept through mile after mile of coastal forest, Jimmy roaring in first gear, riding the clutch, until at last they lurched around a corner, and there, gasping with relief, Molly saw the water she'd dreamed of. The sheet of colour sparkled brightly, putting to rest any frustration she might have felt earlier on towards Jimmy. She tingled, for how different it was to the water the ship had passed over. Then it was more a passage of time, fathoms deep and detached from any continent, a watery substance to push against, the ship like an island for the honeymooners journeying into the unknown. Here, the water in all its blue, cut-glass beauty, belonged to the land, the curves and headlands and rocky outcrops, the two bodies fastened together with a zip of sand and froth, harmoniously attached and symbiotic.

Molly held her chest tightly.

The wheels of the car rolled forward in small jerks while Jimmy gripped the steering wheel. He trembled, gazing into the distance too. An oiled fringe hung loosely over his forehead.

"This is beautiful," she gasped. "Look . . . you don't get this in England! We really are here, just as I imagined." But Jimmy wasn't interested, the driving had exhausted him. Molly continued, "Marj was right you know," and she munched on a green apple pulled out from her neighbour's hamper, spraying juice across to his elbow. Joyce's letter had slipped out with the movement, but Molly pushed it back quickly. Joyce was shouting at Molly but Molly couldn't bear thinking about it, not here, not now, not with the ocean in a mellow dance at her feet.

Down a well-worn path Molly kicked little stones with her slip-ons till she reached the white sand. There she took them off. Jimmy left his lace-ups on.

"I'll race you to the water," she shouted at him, her voice lifting with the coastal breeze. She knew he'd follow, the need to be with her was greater than his fear.

With a shoe in each hand, she skimmed across the sand's surface to the frothy border, followed the backwash down the wet slope till it turned, then raced backwards, her toes clipping the foam as she ran up the beach with a fresh wave, laughing with her head thrown back. She raced forwards and backwards with the waves, again and again, her feet and legs bare and wet. With a floral scarf around her head and dark glasses shading her eyes, she felt collected and impenetrable. Nothing could undermine her. Not the wind, nor the water, nor Jimmy watching from a short distance with his hands in his pockets, her husband, separated out like oil.

"You'll get too ttttired," he shouted at her. "That's child's play, Rosy d—dear. Let's gggg–ggg–go for a walk. Come on."

He started off across the hardened sand far enough away

from the lapping surf to be safe, his brown leather shoes leaving exaggerated patterns with each step. The handcrafted soles had flowers carved into the leather. Oversized cubist flowers. On the sand they took the form of rough potato prints.

Molly caught up, breathless.

"Oh come on, be a sport and wait for me. This ocean and sand is divine. And your shoes look silly." Jimmy continued to plant his line of roses along the sand, one in front of the other, while she swung her shoes in her hands from side to side, her eyes scanning the water as it rose and fell. "Don't be a wet blanket Jimmy," she said. "Not today, not when we've decided to do this together before you go away." In this place, she felt bold, able to talk with Jimmy in a way she found impossible to do back in Canberra.

Debris lay in arcs along the sand, tracing the shape of the waves which broke onto the beach in groups of seven to dump the ocean litter, up and down, up and down. And as the tide had turned, each group crept imperceptibly up the beach in swirling patterns of lace and froth and treasure. There were arcs of tiger-striped shells in blacks and greys, weightless white cuttlefish, polished pebbles and pink crab legs. There were seaweed necklaces and beads, and chains of soft rubbery balls knotted around driftwood.

Jimmy pulled his shirt collar up around his thick neck. "Rosy," he called, turning around and wanting her to catch up.

She lagged a little behind, collecting seaweed and pieces of wood that the great Pacific Ocean had spumed and spat out. She picked up transparent apricot and rose coloured shells that never had the chance to form perfectly.

"Jimmy, how are shells made?" Her watery voice drifted in ripples. "Jimmy!" Louder and more insistent. "How does an animal build a shell? Which comes first? The shell or the thing inside?" Molly loved asking him questions like this. He was a scientist after all, a fact she was proud of. Either he knew, and answered; or he didn't know, in which case he bluffed.

He didn't hear her question.

Molly held a roughly shaped paper-thin shell in her hand. It had pinprick holes around the edge. The layers were so thin she could feel her forefinger and thumb on either side, pressing against the sun-baked skin. She squeezed it. Too hard. Too brittle. It broke in two and sharp splinters fell on the sand.

With another, a pinkish one this time and translucent like the one she'd broken, she smelt the sea. Molly held it up at Jimmy's figure, at arm's length. The small shell fitted his large shape. Then, with an eye closed, the other one concentrating on the curved skin, his image disappeared altogether, eclipsed by her full moon. She collected enough of these shells to fill the deep pockets in her dress. Later, she would thread them together with fishing line and fasten them in a necklace, a present for Marj.

Jimmy turned around, his feet planted wide, mouth open expectantly. As she drew closer to him, bending and collecting and dragging things behind her, his deep voice floated on the wind's surface. He said, "This is f–far enough."

The shells clinked against her swinging hips.

She piled her shoes and the collectibles away from the incoming tide and sank immediately into the softness. "You can sit anywhere on sand." She gasped, catching her breath, staring out at the waves and back along the stretch of beach they had walked. It was a discovery. Sitting without discomfort or concern. "It's not a lounge or a garden with grass, where you have to be particular. And not like the rocky beaches at home, where you just never do it. You can really sit anywhere on sand, you just sink into it, a soft shape all of your own." Molly was pleased with her thought, and then as if that gave her the confidence she needed, she added recklessly, "Let's take a dip. The water will be warm."

"Rosy, you c–can't . . . d–don't, this ocean ccccc–ccc–comes from the Antarctic." His eyes watered. He creased his forehead and dug the rose-bottom heels into the sand. "It'll be c–cold."

"Oh God Jimmy, it'll be warmer than at home. This is why we've come here isn't it? There's no one around. It's secluded. The dunes will shield me." If she thought about it, she sensed a note of cruelty in her voice, but was determined not to give in to his fears. And she didn't confess that she had only ever paddled off Padstow as a child.

"You'll ccccatch a cccc–c . . ."

"Cold! It's all mine!"

"You'll gggg–ggg–get wet."

"Yes, I'll get wet. Of course I'll get wet! I'll dry too!"

"What about your ccc–ccclothes. You didn't bring your new bathing c–c–costume."

"I left it in the car. I'll take these off."

"Rosy . . ."

"Yes, there's no one here. Besides, you've got to do it once, to see what it feels like. You said that about coming here in the first place."

"Yes, b–b–but . . . I'm . . ."

"You said yourself, Jimmy, before we sailed, to be brave."

"I won't cccc–cccc–come in and rescue you."

"I know that," she said, her voice softening, "I'll be careful," she laughed softly, reassuring him. It was his mother, Molly recognized the look, the one he reserved for when he talked about her. Molly thought back to when Jimmy told her she reminded him of Ethel. She remembered the heat of his hand lying over hers.

"D–don't go out too far."

"I won't," she said, swatting a March fly Marj had warned her about, "I'll be fine." She smiled.

"I'll watch you," he whispered.

Ah, there, it was what she had thought.

He was looking at her in a particular way.

He'd confessed once, that although he could recite the

newspaper's record word for word, his memory had become fuzzy and distorted. Molly could see. He would pull at the stray threads, teasing out the knots. And then, at a point of clarity, tenuous and slippery though it must have been, he would perk up and with his eyes wide open and watery he would stare at her for a moment. In a flash it was gone and if it wasn't for a sensual thrill that encased her, an unexpected jolt of mutual happiness, she'd swear nothing had happened between them.

And this was one of those moments, Molly without a stitch on, with only laughter clothing her white body and the quivery air between them, and Jimmy, unmoving, his feet planted firmly in the sand. She began to realize that this was familiar territory for her husband, him holding his breath out of habit with his body rigid as he succumbed to small jabs of pain and happiness, unsure, if you were to ask him, which was which.

She ran to the line of surf in a fast retreating corridor of seduction, thrilled at her daring. He made her do it! So did Marj, bless her, with her sense of place. Everything was so easy to do in this country. You just needed pluck.

The sea was almond green, close up. She wanted to let its colour sweep through and around her, washing against her cliffs and fleshy cracks just as it did to the coastline, pounding her waiting skin, its weight against her flesh, the white swirling water enveloping her breasts, neck and shoulders. Body of water against body of flesh and bone. Everything she felt ready to embrace. Everything Jimmy was afraid of.

Molly waded deeper and deeper, the water rising up her legs, then across her buttocks and stomach and up to cover both breasts. It was cold, but once in, once wet, her movement below the surface and out of the wind created a kind of warmth. She trod water for a while—she was quite good at that—bouncing with each green and white wave, rising and falling, and thrashing her arms about to keep balance. The horizon dipped and disappeared, but she wasn't afraid:

her feet could touch the sandy bottom every now and again for support. And she didn't turn for a long time, imagining Jimmy watching her head bobbing like a cork, imagining his anxiety rising and falling in waves of pink heat with each successive minute. She didn't want to upset him, although she could imagine his eyes becoming glassy and remote, his fists clenching white and drawing beads of blood with sharp nails. Later, when she asked him about it, he'd blame himself.

When she was ready, Molly came in, her appetite satisfied and her body numb but strangely warm inside. As she stood waist-deep, half-way in, the waves continued to ride up and down her bareness, her nipples erect in the cool breeze. There was a second skin covering her bareness, her pale body and the foamy water now one, legs wide apart in the bubbles, feet buried in the sand. She could see Jimmy clearly from there, his eyes feeding on her nakedness unashamedly. A rare chance for him, for the walls of the house were too close. But out here, in a hollowed vacant ant's nest, with the dune's protection, her husband indulged his senses without shame, with greedy eyes.

She came in splashing.

He gave her a large handkerchief to dry herself with, and she felt like a child again, coming out of a steamy bath and into the arms of a waiting mother, the two piercing eyes stark against a large white towel. Back then, as now with Jimmy, being in the water felt safer, protected.

Molly shivered with cold in the breeze. A thin film of salt had stuck to her skin as the vegetation did to the sand dunes. The wind dried the water and salt spray to a crust. Refusing to look into Jimmy's eyes, she dressed quickly, her clothes warm and welcoming. She was all clean, white and starched, and ready to swim and float in the ocean again, surprised at how simple and invigorating it was.

"Your body looked dd–ddark in the water. You cccc–cccould be an Aussie you know Rosy." Jimmy talked about the swim over supper that night. To Molly he seemed quite comfortable, conversational. They didn't go back to Canberra, for fear of the dark highway, the treacherous climb. Instead, after an evening spent looking for cheap accommodation, they found a large weatherboard guest-house, well back from the water. Their room opened out onto a verandah so they could hear the ocean thump against the beach all night, the waves weightless in the dark.

The table was laid for dinner, modestly, with a piece of driftwood in the centre the only extravagance, its skin smooth and white.

"I'll tell Marj."

"Of course, tell Marj. You t–tell her everything d–don't you?"

"Not everything Jimmy."

"M–most things."

"Perhaps."

And that's when Jimmy began to talk of home again, in a fluent tongue, about his mother and her having left him. Perhaps it was being with Molly, having her all to himself, or the relief of having the thumping ocean in the background, behind them, a memory. Perhaps it was the food they were about to eat with a mock silver service. Molly wasn't sure. She just let him talk on.

Jimmy said he remembered being afraid of his own voice from that morning onwards, or was that what his nanny had said? He couldn't be sure. In his mother's house, before the accident, the table they ate from occupied the centre of the dining room. On its starched cloth top, places were laid for the small family day and night. Cutlery and crockery never left its shiny white damask surface. They were placed neatly at intervals around the oval. Ethel Brown loved beautiful things and arranged the decorations in her house with an aesthetic eye. She said the way someone lived reflected who they were. The outside was a mirror to the inside.

After the accident, his mother's mother insisted a nanny look after the young boy. From that day, the two of them—Jimmy and his nanny—ate off a wooden school desk in his bedroom. He remembered the desk was pushed up hard against an empty white wall. Mealtimes were shrouded in silence. It hurt to talk. Jimmy said from then on, a nicely laid table with a bowl of fruit or picked flowers or simply a pretty plate as a centre-piece made his heart sag with sadness.

Perhaps it was the way he told her, wanting to look into her eye, his fingers thrumming the table, that made Molly sad too. She was glad the two of them were tucked away in one corner, their backs to the servery. When he stopped talking, with nothing more to add just then, he took to stroking the smooth white skin of the driftwood in the centre of the table. It calmed him, and she found she loved him then.

For dinner they ate rump steak. Jimmy's was under-cooked, rare. In contrast Molly's was well-done, missionary brown. They ate their steak with a regulation pool of tomato sauce. A mixture of overdone long string beans and cubed carrots sat either side of the meat, the floral pattern on the china submerged.

"My skin will always be too white," Molly said, lightening the table talk. "I'll never be bronze. But I'll enjoy the ocean. I like the surprise of the water."

"I ccc–ccc–can s–see!" Jimmy said, stammering, out of his depth again.

Molly sighed and sat limp, watching Jimmy slice the gigantic steak with a serrated knife, its pink watery blood all dribbly. She felt torn suddenly, drawn to him especially when he opened up, but glad too he was going away. She hated his see-sawing moods, the intensity of his body and his steely muscles. Although she once thought it becoming, she hated his groping for words. Would he ever be rid of it? She was losing patience, and picked at her meat, pulling apart the brown overcooked fibres with a fork.

They left for home early the following morning, both of them in an irritable mood. Jimmy had been agitated overnight, pacing the floor, letting out small grunting noises at each turn, while Molly tried to sleep. She tossed and turned in time with the rolling thumping ocean in the background that seemed louder and closer in the stillness of the dark, her dreams a tangle of memory and desire. Before the first sign of breakfast, Jimmy had packed the car. He was ready to drive. Annoyed with his impatience, Molly insisted on seeing the ocean for one last time.

"No I won't g–g–ggo in," he shouted at her. She was trying to push Jimmy down to the edge of the water. She had him around his middle. "Rosy, I won't g–g–go in! You know that." His head arched back over her straining, pushing body. "Molly Rose!!" There was a note of desperation in his voice.

But she ignored his cry. She wanted to wet him. She wanted to bury his feet in the sand and watch his shoes fill with water. She wanted to mock him and tease him about his fears. She wanted to hear the waves roar with her in laughter and derision and pleasure. She wanted to hurt him for enveloping the night with an impenetrable sadness, for only coming to life when he talked about things of the past, for making her dream of her sick mother. It was too much to bear.

"I don't like gggg–gggetting wet. Molly Rose, please." He tried to sound dignified.

"Gggg–ggg–god you're a wet b–blanket, Jimmy," she told him. "As if I cccc–ccc–ould p–push you around anyway." Molly fought him with his own words, in a cruel way. She mimicked him with a stutter, the force of her consonants spraying him with spittle, and stood back to take in his full height, all six foot six of him. "Or undress you."

"Rosy." His shoulders slumped. As he turned to go back to the car, she reached out a hand to touch him, for she could see she'd hurt him, he had his head down, that head she dearly would have liked to have cradled the previous night, but had felt awkward about it.

"Go on. You go," she said in a gentler way. "I'll just have a few more minutes here. I want to get some water and take it home." She paused, and then with more vigour, not caring who heard her, she shouted, "I want to swim in it at home!" But as she bent to the water, her voice dropped and she murmured to herself, "And give some to Marj."

Back in Canberra, Molly divided the ocean water she'd taken as a souvenir. She filled two small perfume bottles, fastened each with a cork, and sat them on her bedroom windowsill, ready to give one of the pair to her friend.

The light trickled through the clear glass from the outside, colouring the brine faintly. The colours reminded her of children's painting books, where brushes of water changed the paper, magically, highlighting a story hidden beneath the surface. She wondered what it would feel like to be underneath a wave, swimming in the body of water before a kick on the sandy floor brought her back up to the surface, and there, looking up and pushing her lids open, she'd feel the rush of water against both eyeballs and air bubbles escaping everywhere from her mouth and nose. When she learned to hold her breath under water, she would do that one day. She'd hold her eyes open without blinking and for long enough, to see the sky reflected in the brim of ocean, in a wash of moving colour, a weight of silence glassy across the surface.

Molly wondered about the Pacific Ocean to which the two bottles belonged: whether it went up and down, brushed against the sand and curled in waves, without her watching. Did the oceans and streams and pools exist without her observing? In a circular way, she then thought of her mountains, the Brindabellas on the horizon. With their sides wet after a summer storm and the hollow parts of the catchment filled with water, they leant up against the sky. With efficiency and grace, they supplied her with pure untreated water for her laundry taps. It was easy to capture the mountains in her mind's eye, the bumps and curves, the sky-gazing trees and carpets of flowers. In her imagination, she was part of the slope, sitting on a flat rock underneath a tree, having puffed and panted with the climb. Marj had told her the mountains were old, and Jimmy that the soils were leached and weary. In any case, they existed in full with a life cycle, consistency and force all of their own. And it was the imagining and dreaming, that gave *her* life.

She laid her wood and seaweed out to dry in the hot sun, then decorated her kitchen shelves and ledges with the ocean's debris.

silent caresses

JIMMY'S ANTICIPATED leaving to head off up north coloured everything he did. And as the time drew closer Molly found she couldn't help but be nervous too, not that she didn't want him to go, for the thought of being on her own thrilled her, and for eight weeks too. In the face of his anxiety, she concentrated on the washing and ironing and cooking. The solution was a good one. Molly had mastered the domestic skills well by now, and bless Marj for showing her the way.

"Will you come over and have tea with us tonight?" Marj asked Molly as they pegged out the washing together, under the one line. Marj's cotton dress ballooned from around her fat legs.

"You mean supper."

"Yes I do, to you." Marj answered softly, touching Molly's fingers over a pair of green shorts.

"It would be lovely Marj. Do you want me to do anything? I could bring over some leftovers I've got . . ."

"No, of course not, I just thought as the men are leaving us, it'd be nice to have a meal together, all of us, before they go, and you can tell Kevin about the trip to the coast. He leaves tomorrow, Jimmy too." The wet clothes billowed into their faces.

"At first light."

"Queensland isn't it? Lucky devil."

"Western Queensland. He doesn't talk about it much."

"Kevin only goes as far as Yass. He likes doing jobs outside Canberra, then a few inside."

"I'll have to ask Jimmy, you know, about tonight. He may refuse." Molly looked back at her house. Since the trip to the coast, she'd become unsteady with him.

"Oh come on Molly, on the last night. I tell you what, I know you're always worried for him, but for this once don't concern yourself. We'll just eat. I've got a great meal worked out. Roast pork in a roll with all the little extras, sticks of crackling and apple sauce, then my best pavlova. With sliced bananas doused in lemon juice to whiten them. And when it's over, you can go, 'cause I know you'll want time together before tomorrow . . ."

"It's not that, it's just . . ."

"Jimmy feels uncomfortable with Kevin, I know, but he doesn't have to talk. Anyway, you like him don't you? I think you two get on well together. He says he's enjoying having somebody fresh next door, that's nice isn't it? So, we'll talk for your Jimmy. You cover for him anyway when he can't get it out, don't fret, I know, I know, nothing misses me much." Marj smiled at Molly, cushioning the starkness.

"Okay, if you think it'll be all right. I trust you."

"Good."

The invitation was the simple part. And so was the beginning of the meal. Molly had entered Marj's house collected and confident. She sat resplendent in a new jade linen dress with black velvet edgings. Her hair was knotted and decorated with perfectly-formed paper roses. By being in a loved one's home, fractious feelings melted away. The food was scrumptious too. One of Marj's best meals. Food always tastes better when prepared by someone else. Molly's appetite was good and she ate well.

But Jimmy cut it short. There was more to eat and so much more to drink. It seemed unfair. She loved talking about the trip to Bawley Point, how she'd swum in the water —Marj called it skinny-dipping—and how she wanted to see more of the lush forest up the escarpment. Molly was in good spirits, conversational, witty and warm. She loved every moment of it, sensing Marj's and Kev's eyes feasting on her, like bees at a honey pot. But Jimmy told his hosts he had packing to do.

"Talk to me." Molly paced the floor later, biting her nails. "TALK TO ME!! JIMMY!! Please say something. What are you thinking?"

The night air was heavy. No breeze.

"Jimmy . . . talk to me, try to . . . please." Her words hovered between them as she ran her hands over her hips. Smoothing the soft material helped to soothe her.

"I cccc–."

"Yes you can, it's only me, you just have to be calm, let it out." Trying to help him, she relaxed her shoulders.

"I cccc–ccan't."

"See, you just did, you've made a start, that's good, now come on, let it out slowly. Slowly. Tell me what you're thinking. Come on now, slowly . . ." She coaxed him as if he were a young child learning to talk.

"He's a . . ."

"Well?" At first she pursed her lips, then tried to take the edge out of her voice. "That's it Jimmy, you're doing well, just fine."

"A a sc–s–scavenger." Jimmy blurted it out.

"Kevin's a scavenger?" Her fingers quivered.

"Yes."

"Feeds off other people?"

"Yes."

A silence lengthened between them. She thought back to the meal, the thin Browns on one side, the fat Waters on the other, and remembered Kevin licking his lips with a grey tongue across a thin pinkish line. He had sat opposite Molly. As he cut up the pork and distributed the crackling, she heard him saying the phrase "Pommy bastard", spitting it out, then roaring with laughter, his neck and torso quivering. It rang around the kitchen, cutting through the oily heat of the roast. At the time she pretended not to hear it, and had laughed and raced on about other things, even though without looking sideways, she sensed Jimmy's colour change to a deep purple. It was as they drank tea, in small sips from the best blue china, that Molly saw Marj lie her hand over Kevin's, his fat fingers curling in response. Marj tamed Kevin.

"It's only playful," she said, wanting to reassure Jimmy as well as cover herself, convinced Marj knew best. "Marj says he's a teddy bear. Kevin just likes laughing at his own jokes and besides Marj says if you're called a bastard here you're a mate. I wouldn't worry about it—he was just talking in general. Besides it's all over now. And you won't see him for ages."

Jimmy nodded faintly as he began to pack his field clothes into a suitcase. He put in leather ankle boots, thick socks, long-sleeved cotton shirts, new shorts, seed garters, hat and sunglasses.

"Don't forget your handkerchiefs. Here I've ironed a collection for you. Have you got enough canvas bags? Field kit? Mosquito net? Soap? You don't need to shave. Toothbrush?"

"Thanks Rosy."

"What about your books? You need them."

"No, I ccc–, I ccc–ccoudn't ccc–ccconcentrate. T–tttoo dark, I won't r–read, I'll watch the stars instead."

"I didn't think you liked looking up into the southern sky, that's why you hated the African trip. You said it was too big."

"I d–don't."

"Well, that's silly then."

"I'll d–do it ffff–fff–for you."

Molly wanted to tell Jimmy to do something for himself for a change, instead of rotating around her. He seemed helpless under this sky, let alone out in the bush where nothing would block its gobbling expanse. She was envious of what he would see, but its vastness would make him sway and dip uncontrollably. It would made him shrink and cower in the shadows of trees away from a burning midday sun. And then at night he'd disappear altogether into the blackness, scorched by the pinprick light of myriad stars. Half of Molly wanted to protect him by holding his shoulders and squeezing them hard with her fingertips. She could shake him to jelly. To strawberry pulp. Then in order to protect him she would hide him inside her, rather than have him expose himself. The other half, in contrast, wanted to watch him shrivel with helplessness and fear. For Jimmy Brown was such a lousy adventurer.

She said, "Take your pillow."

"I will."

Molly laid his feather pillow across the packed suitcase. Jimmy touched it lightly.

"Look here's a clean slip, smells good with the sun. Have you put in your water bottle for overnight? You drink gallons."

"You lll–ll–look after me Rosy, d–d–don't you?"

"Someone has to." Molly could hear Marj saying the same line, with the same tone of voice. She wondered whether the Waters were packing a suitcase for Kevin's trip, together, remembering last-minute things and laying sweet-smelling clean clothes on top of one another. Or whether their fingers were still curled and interlocked. All one. She wondered how they extricated themselves, how much they had to lean on one another to get off the bed.

"Rosy, I'll call it a day. I'm off to bed," Jimmy was saying. Two perfect sentences. His mouth twitched. "Goodnight."

"Goodnight," she said, beginning to undress.

"Oh, I nnnn–need this t–t–tonight." In a flash, Jimmy slid the pillow out and squashed its soft corners into the clean case. He left for his bedroom, hugging the pillow as closely as he would a woman.

a wet green sky

WITH JIMMY gone, Molly tasted freedom.

"Marj, now this is what I call rain." She shouted across the fence, her voice loud enough to be heard above the pelting water on her roof and the rush in the metal down-pipes. The sky was murky. The mountains hidden.

"This'll be quick Molly, over in minutes and never enough to soak into the soil deeply. Were you okay last night, in the end? Jeez you were in good form."

Molly was standing at her own back door, leaning against the green frame. She wore Jimmy's favourite dressing gown —a miniature pack of cards in red and white printed on black rayon—her hands in the pockets, the long dark neck-line loose and open to a tied waist. Her skin was still pink from a morning shower, feet bare and a few drops of rain tickled her toes to make them curl. She wanted to tell her friend she felt torn with Jimmy around; that every gesture and word he spoke made her fray—a rag strung between two continents; that he was determined to maintain his Englishness, his stiff upper lip and sense of decorum at any cost; that she was pleased to be on her own now, able to absorb the colour of this new land in peace; that she desired Marj's company more than anything. Two months alone— eight weeks, 56 days, 1344 hours alone—was heaven.

Marj was on the other side of the fence, sheltered by the wide eaves and trailing vegetation. Over her fatness she wore green and blue flowers in a sleeveless swirl. A full vase. The dress had a gathered circular neckline slung over a cotton petticoat frilled along the edge. The petticoat straps fell down her arms.

The two women watched the rain smother Mount Ainslie in a wet sheet, lost in their own worlds.

Then Marj shouted and laughed all at once, breaking the spell. "It's raining cats and dogs! Come on Molly, let's get wet! Dare you!"

"I'll get wet!"

"Of course you will! Come on. You'll dry."

They ran out into the downpour, on either side of the fence, across the cement paths and onto the cut grass, laughing like children, faces pointed to the sky, bare arms and hands stretched out wide.

"My hair was almost dry after washing it!"

"Not now!" Marj squealed like a young child. "Don't worry, it'll dry again."

"I love it, I just love it." Molly spun around on tiptoe, fingers stretched wide, conscious she was in control of her senses again. "I can't believe how good it all is." She knew by feeling things on the outside, she owned them inside her, in the gut. It was the same as securing Marj's friendship: tasting food cooked and prepared by her neighbour. The eating was all-important. A communion of souls. A feast. "You can get wet here and not care!" she said. "I've never done this before in my life: Mummy would be angry if I told her, which I won't."

They spun around, twirling and whirling.

Molly clapped her hands. Her voice reached a crescendo above the pelt until she let out a gurgled scream of pleasure, her lips in a big smile, water spraying from an open gargoyle mouth, black inky eyeliner running across red cheeks. She ran on the spot, bare feet splashing the sodden grass, stomping, knees up high, Jimmy's soaked dressing gown flapping open to reveal a wide gap. She stretched her arms out on a cross, fists clenched, face to face with the falling rain.

Marj watched Molly's antics from across the fence, dizzy

with her own twirling, a hand flat on her wide hips to steady herself, the other gripping the edge of the bird-bath for support, grinning.

"Molly, you're delirious." She lumbered up to the fence. "Come here, you dear creature. But watch out for the pit," she added, seeing Molly skirt around its edge, "You need to put a fence around that, it's dangerous!"

The two women stood either side of the fence, tears and rain running ribbons and slipping off the corners of their cheeks. They shouted each other's name, simultaneously, and, standing on tiptoe, clasped one another in a strong firm embrace across the fence as if nothing stood between them.

"Marj, I am truly here."

"Yes, you are, you're nowhere else!"

"You know what I mean, I don't feel like a visitor any more."

"You mean, you won't go home."

The rain poured all around them, a quick summer soak, forming pools in their collarbones, sneaking between their breasts and dripping onto their toes. The wet fabric of their clothes clung to their bodies, giving them both a naked form.

"Molly, you haven't got anything on under that dressing gown! I mean nothing!" Marj laughed shrilly, pulling back. "What a hoot, but at least nobody would know. Look at us both, wet through, and it's usually so dry here so you've got to be quick to catch it. And I don't mind saying it now, but only us to enjoy it. Only us. Ha! No other prying jackhammer eye. They'll never know anyway." She laughed again.

Molly licked the rain off her lips. It was cold. Then she said, "But you do know it's because of you." She never thought she'd be so bold.

"I knew it would happen, in time."

"I belong here Marj, despite Jimmy."

"Of course!" Marj replied without hesitation, and then her voice seemed to harden with the thought, "He'll go back Molly, mark my word."

"Go back?" Molly asked quickly, not sure whether she'd heard Marj correctly, "Jimmy go back? Don't say that." She wondered how Marj knew, had Jimmy said something? *She* wanted to be the one to tell, if she could be sure. Molly traced back through the conversations to tease out the meaning of his words, the innuendoes. Yet, it was strange, once articulated between the two women, once known in this way, the idea took a hold of Molly: it made perfect sense.

"He will," Marj was saying, "He can't take the heat or the glare. You can see it in his eyes. And I could never ever, *ever* see him getting wet like this!" She then chortled in a harmless way, and Molly squeezed her arm, daring to believe her friend.

Marj said: "I've done it since I was a little girl, sloshing home in the gutters, my uniform swimming around me and undressing at the back door, to nothing, and Mum wrapping a big towel around my birthday suit. Jimmy doesn't own a birthday suit Molly! Don't wince, I can tell—he should never have come here in the first place. Poms *bath* fully clothed. He'll go back. But you won't—not now."

"He brought me here." Molly wanted to defend him with something, from mosquitoes that bite.

"So he did, and I thank him for it."

Molly let out a big sigh. She suddenly felt cold. Then she said, "Let's go in, Marj, I'll slip through the bottom gate. Put on the kettle for us both will you."

The rain had stopped. Molly broke the hold and walked through the gardens in a big U brushing the wet vegetation and adjusting her dressing-gown.

"I used to watch the sky as a young girl," Marj said, leaning back in her chair, a hand clasping a mug of sweet black tea.

They had both dried and changed clothes; Marj's triple-X gown swam around Molly.

"I love the clouds pushing up and up until they fan out across the sky. Each one feeds into the next." Marj put the mug down, letting her hands do the actions, moving them in circles, round and round, as if they were part of the convection current. Then her movement slowed, and, pressing her thumbs and forefingers together she paused, her arms way above her head as though she'd reached the final note of an orchestral piece she was conducting. "All wispy. Light. Airy pancakes tossed onto the ceiling and left to drip." She concentrated in the way she did when stirring a cake mixture. "A conspiracy going on right before your very eyes. A conspiracy to rain. I used to watch from our verandah up at home, half scared, half mesmerized. Once I was counting like I've taught you, the lightning lighting up the house and everything around it, but I didn't even get to one before diving for the inside screaming, as the thunder shook the house. Dad shouted out: "Shut up, yer bugger, I can't hear the cricket." Not that he could hear anything, the wireless was so crackly. I always thought that was the way I'd die—at the end of a lightning bolt, diving for cover, burnt from the inside out, my fat holding the heat like candle wax. They'd find me in the morning groping for a tree, my feet fused to the ground!"

Molly loved Marj talking: she was fluent in a down-to-earth sort of way. Hard and brittle at first, but a torrent later once she was sure of an audience, the words coming in a rush. It was just like a jug of her smooth warm gravy running out to moisten thickly sliced meat. Was Marj really right? Would Jimmy go home? She wanted to make it hard for him, so he would reach out for her; so she could feel him. And what would his leaving do for her? He revelled in the pleasures of *his* mother country; she didn't. He would fly back into the bosom of the empire, back to safety, to the familiar. He flirted with impossibilities—a lousy adventurer —while Molly Rose Moone, the newly-wed, failed him. Perhaps her breasts were too small, not enough to keep him. She looked with envy at Marj's bosom spilling out over the top of her bodice.

117

As if in a dream Molly said, "I like the sky too Marj." She knew in her heart that he was already there, Jimmy had never really left. "It doesn't rain like this at home." Her eyes were glassy with thought. She had her mother to think of too.

"At home?" Marj was saying, "You'll never be able to go back. Anyway, how could you put up with grey drizzly slosh all year around?"

"I wouldn't," Molly replied, hardly believing what she heard her lips saying. It was one thing to think something, another thing altogether to say it.

"Pour me some more tea, Marj, please, and keep talking." Molly bit her lip, fighting tears, thinking of Jimmy and Joyce and now Marj before her and the enormity of it, how she'd rather not have to decide between them all, not yet. At least Jimmy was away for a time, that made things simpler, but there was Joyce in hospital, this much Molly knew, but it wasn't clear what was wrong. Her mother's letters were muddled and confusing. And there was nothing Molly could do—not that her being in hospital drew her closer, if anything, it put a deeper chasm between them, underscoring their separation, their difference. Molly found herself not believing her mother: sadly, from when she was a little girl she realized she never had. Joyce had written: *You don't care do you? I am in hospital. I don't like them in here—too rushed —too rude—why can't I go home. Remember how I used to fly out to a smell of pigeon manure and straw—my smell—all over. I'm back in time for breakfast it doesn't pay to be gone when they come in the door and I eat hot buttered toast and honey and black tea. I see it all as I go a thousand tall steel chimneys billowing with smoke and the noise and clamour of hundreds of beds and the nasty cylindrical trolleys filled with the dead trundling to the morgue. The sun shines ever so weakly like watered down parsnip soup from the day before . . .* and later . . . *I had a funny thought the other day. What have you done with those pearls I gave you? You couldn't possibly wear them over there, far too hot. They would make your pretty neck sweat and go grey and that would be terrible.* Molly had tried writing back in order to ease the pain. It was more to know she'd done something, rather than believing it would do any good.

"Well," Marj was saying, "After the thunder comes the rain." She lifted the ragged woollen tea cosy. "It makes the drought and the waiting bearable. Lie low and wait is what I've always said, for there's always a feast. If you wait long enough, you'll get fed in the end. I love the big hearty drops, the ones that hit and spray across the gravel surface or bounce if it's hail. Our garden would brighten with an eerie sort of light, flicking through the vegetation. Mind you Canberra's not like Queensland—there it drips *every* day!"

Molly sipped the tea.

Marj said, "One day, I'll take you to Queensland—then you'll know you're alive!—now that you've decided to stay. You can do so much more once you are here for good you know."

Molly drained her cup, spitting back a few stray black leaves.

With the men away, Marj and Molly would eat their meals together, and later drink tea under a fan, telling one another stories. That night Molly stayed over until it was time for bed, then slept with visions of twirling bodies in a sea of rain. Holding hands they swirled together around a garden, a pink bird-bath as a centre-piece. She dreamt of a dreamy Marj, her breasts a soft and luscious brown. Molly was close to clothing herself with that skin, on the edge of imitating Marj.

119

twirling without confusion

OFF THE Sunshine Coast, Mudjimba Island lies low in the Coral Sea. Mudjimba, the Old Woman, Molly's Marj. If she could just keep her eyes focused . . .

She'd slipped a toe in under the film of wet sand. Pools of water were always close to the surface . . .

And this is the best part of remembering the past, the twirling without confusion. A frozen frame.

After the night's storm the water had looked cold and uninviting, she wouldn't go in. How much she'd changed, growing acclimatised to the Queensland sunshine and its harsh summer heat. She was a sucker for warm surf, the sort that encased the body. Only southerners and eager children and *new* migrants! were brave enough to go in on a day below twenty-five degrees. Jimmy wouldn't know her! She smiled affectionately at the thought of him, a little tug at the corners of the mouth. He was rather decent in an unmoving kind of way. She ground her toes further into the seeping pool, thinking of how poorly she'd treated him back then, so that her feet disappeared beneath the soggy heavy sand. The tide was on its way out as she stood there for a time, caught between the act of going and staying, footless and anchored to the long empty beach—Mudjimba Beach —staring sightless across the flat surf that lapped and rolled its way down the face of the sand in long lines of grey and white, to the island, lying low.

Keep your eyes focused Molly.

Oh yes, the twirling of bodies under a wet green sky.

This twirling, this whirling. Rolling rings of flesh. Being on the edge of imitating Marj, her Australia. That was the point of it all. A frozen frame. Before the confusion.

stuttering postcards

"MARJ, I'VE done it," Molly said, running up the back steps under the leafy banksia rose. She looked agitated.

"Done what? Here, you can help me with this." Marj handed her a wooden spoon. "Get another egg will you, I'm doing a sixer. It's the beating—if you beat enough, the mixture never has a chance to lose heart and deflate, it's got that much much air in it."

"I've made up a pattern for you to go with the material I had," Molly said, tapping the spoon on the table. There was something else on her mind.

"Hope it doesn't make me look fat!"

"I'll cut it out this afternoon off my block. Shaped. Padded shoulder to accentuate your line. Buttoned front. Lace camisole peeking out at your bust. You'll look lovely." As she spoke Molly's body slowed down, she stopped tapping the table, her eyes concentrated on Marj.

Marj said, "Molly, this is more than I've ever worn."

"You've never had me sew something for you, and you've never had a daughter marry. Things change." A wisp of fear tugged at the corner of Molly's eye. If Marj had stopped working on her sponge to touch Molly's arm, it would have been like steel. Molly's agitation was that close to the surface.

But Marj was intoxicated with her beating and the thought of a new frock. She whipped the wooden spoon, the flap of her arm swaying in time. "Does the money cover it?" she asked.

"Yes," Molly responded breathless.

"It's the best?"

"Yes of course."

"Shoes?"

"Your old comfortable slip-ons."

"Corset?"

"Yes. Definitely."

"Suspender belt?"

"Yes."

"Stockings?"

"See-through and silk."

"Silk?"

"A present from me Marj, to say thank you for everything, we've got the money."

"You shouldn't you know, you should keep your money for when you need it."

"I insist Marj. You'll look lovely, they've got seams up the back of the leg." Molly was rocking now from foot to foot.

"Hat?"

"Of course, I'll use scraps."

"What shape?"

"Large to balance the shoulders, or else you'll look like a wrestler. I want the shape of a thumbtack, big, but light. Flowers and material on its brim."

"Fresh ones?"

"Yes, from your garden."

"What colour?"

"Cream—eucalyptus flowers or something. You've got so many to choose from."

Marj asked, "What are you wearing on your head Molly?"

"A feathered curvette," Molly said, "But . . . I've got something else to show you."

"Get me the cloth Molly dear, no, the one near the oven, warming, there's a dear. What do you want to show me then?"

"Marj . . . Jimmy's going home . . ."

"See, I told you. But how do you know?"

"Look at this." Molly threw a post-card onto the floury table surface. On one side of the card was a drawing of a flower in scratchy crayon lines.

"A Cooktown orchid . . ." Marj murmured and turned it over.

Molly watched Marj feast on Jimmy's words:

Sick with infected mosquito bites and grass seed. Fever. Eating shot pig roasted. Soil's too hard. Broke my shovel. Red raw from the sun. I've made up my mind.

Marj said, "He's sick. Why didn't he wear those protectors you made him?"

"Must have forgotten, or the grass was too high. It was his best shovel too," Molly added. "His favourite. They gave it to him when he started work."

"Could be a momentary lapse, Molly. It doesn't actually say what he's decided to do. He could have made up his mind over anything. We don't know for sure." Marj seemed reluctant to accept the card. She folded in a cup of flour, glancing at the recipe, licking her finger with approval.

"It's obvious."

"I can hear him stuttering in this card."

"Marj . . . He's not." Molly defended Jimmy. She wanted to be the first to talk so freely. *She* had the right to say it, not Marj. "He should write things down more often." Molly toyed with an authoritative voice.

Marj took her hand in reply.

"What will I do Marj, what should I do? I can't write."

"Ask at his work."

"No I'd never do that. Jimmy's never involved me there. That's *his* world."

"Then wait." Marj snapped, frustrated. She pulled away and slipped her mixture into the hot oven.

"Okay okay okay." Molly turned away too, abruptly.

"Molly, I'm sorry."

"Okay. I just hope he's all right. I'm worried," she said, wanting to turn and face Marj, wanting to confess that she was more concerned about herself than Jimmy. If he were to go, where would that leave her? She remembered walking down the street in the early days, after she had dared take off her stockings. A warm wind blew around her skirt and petticoat, caressing her legs. Being bare, the warmth of the air felt like another piece of clothing, a thin silky coat, except it was so close, so fitted, so well cut that it stretched over her skin with ease, without a seam or dart or any bulk. It was like a warm body suit, its touch was that real. She'd felt she belonged, but now she wasn't so sure. She wanted to step into that body suit again, feel its touch, but was afraid: it was slipping through her fingers. Marj was too hard.

"I *am* sorry, I *do* understand." Marj held her elbow, lightly. Molly shuddered with some relief. "You don't have to decide yet you know," she said. "You've got another month or so. Here, come with me."

They stood together in Marj's pink and white glass bathroom. Marj sloshed water and lavender soap over her hands, cleaning the flour and egg from under her fingernails.

"Molly, do you know Barb's told me I've got to lose some weight? I saw her at Civic today."

The comfort and ordinariness of Marj's words made Molly feel warm again. She said, "The green linen is big enough. It'll fit you Marj."

Could the silky suit—that warm body suit she'd once felt—stretch over her skin again? No seams, no gusset, no zips.

the notebook

THE WAYSIDE rest area fills with a cool wet mist and a whitened stillness. Everything is formless, dislocated and silent, waiting for the veil to lift, for the forest to take shape.

It is very early.

She wakes, her neck stiff and crinkled. The girls lie in a tight motionless ball in the back, head to toe, under a blanket.

A dry sclerophyll forest calms her. There, everything is in its place, sparse, and with enough light and spaciousness to see the sky through the open canopy. After all it was part of her first impression of the wide brown openness of the land.

But this . . .

Too tired to drive on, they had camped by the roadside on the Putty Way past Singleton. Through the night, beyond the limits of the sedan (the windows and doors were locked) was nothing, a black hollow that even eyes couldn't adjust to, but at the same time a feeling of being watched by a clutter of trees and vines and thick branches.

Out there past the metal protection.

Pressing in against the duco.

She had slept in fits, the fourteen-hour drive taking its toll. As she woke, a strange sticky sensation, a bitterness, lay across her tongue. She wanted to spit it out but felt she had to accept it like a measure of medicine. And now, the white eerie ghostliness of a new morning makes her want to open the windows on the car's fuggy interior—a mixture of leftover fruit, sleepy body smells and clammy mouths, teeth furry with stale fruit—to move, quickly, south-west, to safety.

Or does it?

There's something protective too about this sensual silence, where even the birds are unaware of the nearing sun. And she doesn't yet know, for sure, whether the dry open forest is as safe as she once supposed on those walks up the flank of Mount Ainslie.

She knew she would go back. She'd been waiting for something, hadn't she? And it didn't make sense to wait for nothing: you had to wait for something to give the waiting meaning. She'd go back when she was ready, she told herself repeatedly, and this line was easy to argue because she was never fully prepared. How quickly her courage ebbed and flowed, pushing her from a point of near departure to that of retreat.

She is a mother now—a single mother—to fourteen-year-old twin girls. Marj will be pleased. In 1974 it was, at the age of thirty-three or so—it's never too late. The first-born is called Kate, and the second (fraternal) born twenty minutes later as a complete surprise (they thought it was the placenta), is Sarah. Joyce bred pigeons while she mothered: the daily ritual of cages, fluff and pellet food kept her focused. But for the next generation, migrant and mother in Australia, the only child grown into an adventurer, the new mother abandoned by the father because of the double surprise, it isn't a flock of birds that keep her alive, but numerous notebooks. Lists and lists and LISTS. She'd written: *Tidy beds, sweep verandah, water pots.* Big lists and small one-liners. *Buy cleaning fluids.* In blue and red ink. And:

> *Look up migrant = one who migrates. Migration = chemical, a change of place . . . (that's better) . . . a movement of atoms, ions, or molecules? . . . Make jelly from box of quinces (look up recipe in CWA). Use peanut paste jars.*

All through these years she has been caught in the whirl of an eddy. By denying herself the luxury of reflection, she survives the rush of day-to-day living and the bringing up of two beautiful girls on her own.

She will tell Marj about her invention. She is a good mother, a great manager, thanks to the pen and paper she tucks into the empty xylonite saltcellar hanging on a hook above the stove. She's written everything down, all the details of everyday life, the humdrum of domestic housewifery. And what keeps her burning inside, is the rest, her precious past, a murmuring Canberra summer and the wide brown legs of Marj with the complementary bulging white triangle, the wet green sky with the swirling and twirling, and the beating of eggs. She has kept these obsessions in her head, and *never* does the rigour of everyday life, the repetitive tasks, the numerous tiny decisions that accompany growing children, clog her mind and so eclipse these memories, these infatuations.

The two—present and past—never mixed. Until now.

She'd written:

General method for jelly making: fully matured, not over-ripe fruit. Boil fast (with enough water to cover) till fruit is soft; strain through clean calico cloth (run through, don't press, for clear jelly). One cup of sugar for every cup of liquid. Boil till it jells.

It seems she has been waiting in the mist for almost three decades, for this moment, the setting point. Waiting to be transformed.

Skim carefully any scum that rises.

The rising scum makes Molly think of the heat and trickle of sweat, and the red fat arms stirring with a wooden spoon. Marj never wasted anything. The creamed frothy jelly top—the scum—was reserved for later, to eat with dobs of yellow butter on biscuits. Loquat jelly was a favourite.

Watch that the jelly doesn't burn. Test before bottling.

Canberra lies to the south, four or five hours' drive away,

ready to take shape; she can't go back to Queensland now. It's too late anyway, for the syrup has jelled, a tacky vermilion ball lies at the bottom of a glass of cloudy cold water.

loquat jelly lips

MARJ'S LIPS were the colour of the finest loquat jelly that summer. From a jar her friend gave her, Molly spread the syrupy mixture onto buttery toast each breakfast.

The night before Kevin arrived home from a fortnight in Yass, the two women drank hot black tea together. The ceiling fan whirred. As they parted, Molly licked Marj's transparent-red lips in a nip of a kiss. Loquat jelly lips. Sugary sweet and sticky.

PART TWO

a family portrait

WITH HER first small lemon tucked hard into her chest, Molly ran into Marj's house as best she could, her tall heels clicking precariously across the concrete. She had watched the lemon grow from a white flower into a lime green, then yellowish fruit. Now, she could cook with her own lemon. She would try one of her friend's favourite recipes: lemon chiffon pie—a sweet fluffy filling in a shortcrust pastry case. She'd garnish it with piped whipped cream and a curl of candied lemon skin. Her lemon skin. And they would have afternoon tea together with the best china and embroidered tablecloth, washing the food down with hot black tea. Besides that, Molly wanted to show Marj her new stilettos bought especially for Barbara's wedding. They were the colour of avocado pears, black and green, with sweetheart bows on their heels.

The Waters' house was still hot on the inside.

The cool change had come through with a refreshing drink of rain and wind. The temperature plunged during lunch. Magpies gurgled in a clump of scribbly gums. But inside Marj's red-brick, three-bedroom house, the heat of the past week was trapped.

Running with the lemon close to her chest and careful not to trip, Molly remembered the last storm, her embrace with Marj across the paling fence and their being pleased it was water, not juice that fell from the sky! Rain is more agreeable, but without the refreshing piquancy the juice of a lemon can give. She wished it would pour from the sky now, in celebration of her one piece of fruit from a young tree, in celebration of her coming to Australia, calling it home, and learning to cook lemon chiffon pie. *You can do so much more once you are here.*

The change had to be enjoyed with Marj, who anticipated and talked about it coming from the south-west like an old familiar friend. Marj described the things she loved in detail. She rolled her wet tongue luxuriously around the syllables, before swallowing and eating the feast of words. Molly wanted to walk up Mount Ainslie with Marj at dusk and talk about the beading for Barbara's veil. The white tulle edged with tiny cream pearls billowed in her mind.

She paused outside the Waters' home.

The heat was like fat caught between skin and bone.

"Marj?" A deep sleepy voice called from the master bedroom. "That you?"

Flies crawled over the wire of the red metal meat safe, fat brown blowflies and midget black bush flies, attracted by the heat and smell of a kitchen and a screen door left open, carelessly. A plate of cold roast lamb, half eaten, was on the top shelf under a wire cake cover. Usually Marj was cautious with meat. She'd slip it into the refrigerator, saying nothing was worse than maggots crawling around in a good cut. A flypaper dangled haplessly.

Molly smelt Kevin in the house.

"Marj!"

Molly wondered where she was. Washed dishes glistened on the wooden rack. Her tired housecoat, the one with the pretty glass buttons, lay thrown over a chair. The bride's mother's list of THINGS TO DO hung above the sink, pinned to the curtain. A pot of tea stood on the table accompanied by cups and saucers, half empty, cold dregs from morning tea. The milk had separated from the water and was lying in a film of concentric circles on the surface, staining the white china with a rim of brown scum. This was not the Marj Molly knew. And she remembered Marj saying life was calmer when Kevin was away, more ordered.

Uneasy, Molly shuffled back across the lifting lino, click, click, click, the lemon still squashed between her breasts. She'd come back later.

Too late.

Kevin was there, at the door to the hallway, licking dry lips, his fingers plastering the wooden frames. His watery eyes drifted in a rose-pink blush. Large underpants, stained yellow, hugged his lower half, the fine brushed cotton stretched and misshapen with wear, hanging over meaty thighs. His chest was bare save for two purple orchids with red centres tattooed on either breast. His fatness spread the colours thinly.

"Uhm, it's only me." Molly waved her arms about, trying to imagine Kevin in a black dinner suit for the wedding with a red carnation pinned to his lapel. Marj worried she'd never get a suit big enough, so a special order had been made at Fletcher Jones. "Sorry to disturb you," Molly said hurriedly, "I'll come back later. Tell her I called . . ."

"Well, if it isn't the pretty lovely from next door." Kevin coughed, regaining his composure. Pulling up his underpants, he said, "Our family owes a lot to you."

"Look, I'm sorry to disturb you . . . your rest . . ."

"You're not disturbing me in the least." Kevin gesticulated with his arms, spraying them away from his body in a wide circle, hitting the sides of the door. "There's no need to go, I'm just sleeping off last night and the little woman'll be home . . . soon . . ."

"You were sleeping . . ."

"You're Marj's friend, so you're *my* friend." He dropped his voice, caressing the words.

"I'm busy at home." She looked again at the cold tea in the stained cups. Marj usually washed up after tea.

"Are you now?"

"I've got some sewing to do. Beading. Hems."

"And what if I don't believe you, my pretty," Kevin's fat hands fell on his hips.

"Please . . ."

"Well," he responded in a soothing voice, "Stay awhile." He moved towards Molly in short confident steps. "Keep me company, poor old Kev. I've just got home and haven't seen you for a long time. Marj'll be here as I said. You'll see her soon. Kev's promise. Anyway you've caught me haven't you, looking like this? Even my daughter hasn't seen me like this. Marj says she's so happy since you've moved in. I haven't seen enough of you, or that husband of yours. Both kids, makes me realize how much of our lives have already gone." His blue eyes drifted again, all over her, as he clenched and unclenched his fist.

"No look . . . I don't . . ." She began to feel uncomfortable without anything to hide behind. She backed towards the door, running her sweaty hand across the wooden tops of the chairs tucked into the table. With Marj, her hands didn't tremble, but with Kevin . . . it was his eyes . . . And then, suddenly without blinking, she was on the floor. Her new high heel, one of those ever-so-small points on tall champagne-glass stems, had clipped a crack in the lino; the ankle flipped to one side while her lemon rolled and took cover.

"See . . ." His voice sang softly.

"Damn," she said, her body collapsing without the support of a leg. She cursed herself for her shoes and her vanity, for the heat and the cool change, for Jimmy's field work, for Barbara's wedding—the pastel gowns hanging from her bedroom picture rail—for being curious about Kevin and his see-through eyes, for deciding to visit Marj with the gift of fruit (it was too little and green and sour anyway), for even coming to Australia in the first place.

In his eagerness Kevin spread his body over the floor, kneeling close to the discarded two-tone stiletto, and reached for her bare foot.

"You can't go now. We'll have to nurse this. Here, I'll help you." He lifted her leg, his warm hand clasping her cold foot. Her dress rode up past her knee while she tried to remain decent, holding one arm over her chest and the low neckline, the other clasping the table for support. Where was Marj's dark shadow filling the back doorway with armfuls of groceries? Where was the order? Routine? Molly's lips were parched and dry, stretched wide and colourless. She cowered, involuntarily pushing the cotton fullness of her red dress and loose petticoats between her legs. Kevin pressed her whiteness with fat fingers.

Then with one lift, in silence, he picked her up above his stomach and chest and swung her through the hall to the master bedroom. Molly had never seen this far before. All the talking she and Marj had done had been out the back of the house, in the kitchen or laundry, or on rare occasions, in the bathroom. Through the door of the hallway, the rest of the house remained silent, beyond the edges of consciousness. And here was Kevin carrying her into that inner sanctum. A family portrait, framed with brown wood and identical to the one in the kitchen lined the mantelpiece, four boys and Barbara. Otherwise the room was bare, the double bed the only furniture. He laid her on the bed, as if he cared, gently.

"Marj likes you. You can rest here," he said, puffing his huge chest to double the size in one intake of air. Then he sat on the side of the bed, the mattress and her thigh slipping in under his rump like melted butter. It warmed Molly, growing imperceptibly into a reluctant but certain stain of body heat.

And he touched her. Stroked her.

She wanted to cry out, I'm all right, I'll go home. But her mouth opened and shut without a sound.

"I'll just do what Marj would do," Kevin was saying. "She'll be proud of me, you'll see. Just close your eyes."

There, it could hardly be plainer, that was it: *I'll do just what Marj would do, she'll be proud of me.* Was that what he really said, or a reprogramming of the words to fit into the motion picture Molly is directing, the frame by frame description? At the time he would have been hard to argue with, he was so huge. Indeed in her memory he'd doubled in size, as if Marj and Kevin had become one great body of flesh, a mutation of desire and longing. Of course it had hurt, that kind of cruelty in pleasure will always hurt; she'd learnt that since then during those years in Queensland. Your sex is the one thing you have that you can call your very own, and yet how easy it is to give away. Back then, holding his body in her hands, with everything she had, with might, certain she was pleasing her friend yet struggling to breathe as his saliva lapped around her lips, she knew she wouldn't be sure till she saw Marj again and heard the whispering tones of support and comfort in her dear voice. But that was such a long way off.

Limping in snatches, she'd stumbled home with an ankle three times its size, bruises all over, and a pair of useless shoes in her hand. Kevin Waters had gone by then, and his house was silent. But she smelt him in her skin. She felt those milky worms over her body again, in sticky clumps, the ones that had visited her in dreams. What was new was the smell of moving flesh, seeping and stale. And the irony was, she'd never smelt it before.

Behind locked doors and drawn blinds, she ran a hot bath in the blue and black bathroom. There, alone, she became walled in by darkness, safe and stiff. She'd stripped off her clothes and jewellery to find a pearl earring was missing, one of the pair Jimmy had given her. In the confusion it must have fallen off, but she couldn't go back to retrieve it. Would Jimmy notice if she didn't wear them any more? Would Marj find it? God forbid! Molly's aching legs and feet swam in the sweet warm water splattered with eucalyptus and lavender oil—presents from Marj—alongside bruised floating breasts. Limp strawberry blonde hair lay across the water-line and swirled below the surface, gossamery seaweed. The bath overflowed. The water lapped over the high enamel sides forming puddles on the cement floor. The slow trickle of hot water from the tap emptied the tank. She couldn't get enough.

As she buried herself, submerging her skin and her tears, she thought of Marj and the last time they were together, kissing beneath a swirling fan, how she caught her friend's loquat lips between her own. The taste of *sweet sweet* jelly. But she couldn't bear thinking about it now. She couldn't go back to find what was lost. Molly wanted to be alone.

The bath water went lukewarm, then cold. Rings of soap and oil lay in bubbly piles on the surface. Molly's toes and fingers wrinkled and bulged like soaking prunes.

a frosted glass of milk

THE SCENT of jasmine leaked through the kitchen door in the early evening. It should have been a comfort, but it reminded Molly of home. Jasmine was a smell her mother hated; one she said should be kept in small bottles with gold mesh squeezers for expensive looking women to splash and spray under their pouchy cheeks. What would Joyce think now, of her little girl? Molly could see her with the garden shears in hand, pruning the neighbour's jasmine back to a claw for daring to drop over the fence, with a look of tribal triumph in her eye.

Molly, the little girl, had been caught in the bedroom once, undressed to the waist while twirling a nipple with her nimble fingers. She remembered Joyce's white satin face with the same look in her eye, her small hand being slapped hard, and the screaming, about how it was for marriage, for when a woman came of age with a man. In secret, the young Moone girl enjoyed wiping her chest; feeling the swelling lumps, intrigued by their suppleness, whiteness and nipple-pink ends. Each month she massaged them, tantalized by the feeling of heat over the rest of her body, sensitive to a blush, drawing the skin out to the tips. She massaged her breasts enough to draw out sap, weak yellowing milk, enough to make them wet. They flopped and bounced as she ran. Looped in curves when she bent over. Formed clefts and cleavages and humps. Until Joyce snapped one day and covered them up in white cotton trainer cups with wide straps. Joyce told her that girls with breasts get into trouble.

Trouble. Was that the word for it?

First Jimmy, then Kevin, two extremes.

Jimmy ate her naked breasts from afar, then curled his warm interior in upon itself. While Kevin swam all around and all over in a mass, licking up her whiteness with a wide prickly tongue, till she bled.

Before sleeping and to steady herself, Molly drank from a tall glass of milk. She sat at the kitchen table in the dark with her sore foot on a chair. A bowl of Queensland nuts kept her company. Hard box-brown balls. Smooth. Full moons. Marj had taught her how to lay them in a dip in the cement and crack them cleanly with a hammer, one blow, dead centre. You crack open the smooth shell, hold the creamy nut flesh between index fingers and thumbs, and split the nut apart into two sheer cross-sections. Marj gave her neighbour a bagful from up north.

Moonlight crept through an open window. The nuts huddled in the shadow cast by Molly's body, untouched.

Distracted, her fingers tracing over the frosted bumps of the glass in her hand, she wondered what had happened in the Waters' bedroom. Did it bring them all a little closer? Why didn't she bite Kevin with her white teeth, the way Jimmy bit, to draw blood? Why did she have to black out? Another mouthful. Milk dripped from the corners. She'd felt so heavy, lying on the custom-made bed, her foot in agony. Kevin's eyes—or were they Jimmy's?—sucked at her pink salty flesh. And there, above her, was his flabby cheek. She could never open her mouth and sink her teeth into that, press her teeth hard enough to draw blood, to bite and eat, enough to tear the flesh, to taste Kevin's body in her mouth between her lips. A body kissed by Marj! She wiped her milky mouth on her dressing-gown sleeve and loosened the bodice over her sore, hot breasts. Her mind was playing tricks: she wanted to please Marj by pleasing Kevin. But her breasts were on fire. Barbara's nearly-finished bridal gown hung from the doorway. It was pure like fresh milk with its low scalloped neckline and layers of cream and white Chantilly lace and tulle. Marj would be pleased. With the last mouthful from the bottom of her frosted glass, she thought of all the dresses she had sewn for weddings, and of the suit in which she married Jimmy—a plain brown wool suit, fitted to the shape of her body, with a single string of pearls for her neck and Jimmy's matching earrings for her ear lobes. Jimmy— her husband—why he'd never touched her breasts, in the raw, naked, flesh against flesh. He only devoured them from afar, crying out in pain. It was Kevin who'd introduced her to carnal pleasure, at her expense. Mouth to mouth. Openings everywhere. All she wanted was to be like Jimmy, and curl into a ball to protect her moist insides.

sticky flies

HANGING FROM the ceiling of Molly's kitchen next to the length of crackly fluorescent tubing was a flypaper. The small blue canister with its long yellow tongue hung by a fragile thread. The kitchen was unremarkable in other respects. She never thought to remove or replace the sticky treated paper. She didn't think you had to: that the stickiness would lose its stick, that the predatory attractiveness would fade. The flypaper floated in the kitchen, buoyed by greasy fumes, crowded with unfortunate corpses. All greasy and yellow and sticky with flies, it kept the young woman's house free of the flying pests, her surfaces free of germs. Ugly and unseemly, but useful, essential. Grotesque but beguiling.

Thinking back on her first impression, it was the pesky fly she remembers most, with disgust. Marj had said in her caring way, "They only land on you when they're hungry and starving and looking for food." You think you'd never get used to the way flies flirted with your body, crawling over the sweaty skin. Prickly threads like the hairy jointed legs of a housefly tickle and itch her memory. For what she remembers of that unhappy day was his appetite and the speed with which he fed it; swallowed and devoured in a gulp, as she watched small black flies dance in pairs above the bed. The flypaper swings in her memory. The curious thing is, she'd never seen a flypaper since. Marj had set it up for her as a neighbourly gesture.

How could she forget the way the flies persecuted her over that first summer, never leaving her alone? Nothing but a whingeing Pom they would have said had she uttered a protest. Now, apart from Sarah's school project about the pesky creatures, Molly doesn't even notice flies. What flies she says? *Oh them, yeah, they only land on you when they're hungry and starving and looking for food.* Sarah had many school projects but the one Molly remembers was on the life cycle of a fly. They were living in Nambour in an old Queensland house on tall stilts, with a wide airy verandah and wrought-iron trim. The underneath of the house with its hard sandy floor was a perfect place for projects. All manner of activities were transferred out of the upstairs rooms and down the ricketty clatter-bang stairs. Amongst clumps of ripening bananas, potted cuttings ready for planting, and second-hand furniture Molly was keen to strip back, there was a corner devoted to the girls' play and their projects. Not counting the early days in Australia, it was the happiest Molly had ever been. They lived there for six years altogether, until Molly lost her job and had to move to the coast.

Sarah's school project on the fly covered every available space under that house. Its beginning was quite accidental, a brainwave after a picnic in the back garden with cold chicken and lettuce sandwiches. Molly had stupidly left the chicken unwrapped, and there, beneath the crackling brown oven-baked skin of a size sixteen Farmland special, the chicken's white meat merged in colour with an army of marauding maggots. Disgusted but fascinated, Molly wrote in her notebook:

> *flies liquefy their food, then suck it up with mouths shaped like funnels*
> *the female lays hundreds of eggs at one time and within hours maggots emerge to feed*
> *maggot = 1. the legless larvae of a fly, living in decaying material*
> *2. an odd fancy, a whim*
> *a female housefly can lay 250 eggs*

The maggots were a godsend. The end-of-year science projects had to be finalised, fast. Sarah (the twin thought to be a placenta, who dresses in vintage clothing from op shops) was keen on anything that moved, so the maggots were a hit. And the notebook from the saltcellar became very useful indeed; it drew mother and daughter even closer together. They researched the project side by side.

larvae eat whatever they hatch on

larva is a Latin word meaning a ghost or mask

The two of them watched the maggots grow fat, the skin of the beasts strangely translucent and ringed.

larvae eat and grow fat, then spin skins

Strange she should think of that project now. And the gift of the flypaper.

inedible dreaming

THAT NIGHT, Molly dreamed. On the migration ship, a body bag had been thrown overboard. It fell in a belly flop onto rolls of water below. It fell with a crash with a nest of rocks hidden in the sailcloth helping it to sink. And as she dreamed, drifting in and out of sleep and disappearing in and out of the bathroom—nauseous, vomiting, a terrible headache—Molly rose and fell with those waves overpowered and nearly drowning too. She longed to be washed ashore, to safety, to a place of resurrections. The morning took forever to get there.

She dreamed . . . *Jimmy is swimming,* God bless him, *out deep, calling,* she could only see his hand, *calling a name, a wave between. The surf rises and falls with the swell, interrupting his stuttering with a roar. He calls a perfect name— Rosy, Rosy . . .* And Molly lay nestled in the fold of a white sheet, not wanting to lift her head from the bank of embroidered pillows, her head exploding, her stomach aching, a taste of bile on her tongue. She lay as still as she could, with no strength to get dressed, the blinds drawn. . . *Jimmy holds a clump of spent red camellias across the turbulent water. Brown edges, worn out, torn. He brings them close, in a surge, the petals touched brown with fingers . . . you love me, you love me not, you love me, you love me not . . .* and Molly imagined the old woman, the one from the bingo game, sinking out deep, all zipped up with the rocks pressing into her stiffened flesh. Somewhere on the ocean's floor she would come to rest and the captain of the ship would have to explain to her relatives how it was simpler that way.

The morning came and the sky changed colour from blue to sun-bleached white, the sun puncturing the night air. Close to her body, summer flies had begun the day with vigour, buzzing and dancing over the misshapen bed. But the light made no difference, for out of exhaustion, Molly lay on the dishevelled bed, and with her eyelids closed she let those dreams surround her again, as if willing them to her side. She'd entered a dangerous and disturbing world; even so, it beckoned.

She dreamed . . . *the new neighbours sit around in a semi-circle on canvas furniture, their mouths tied with gags, blindfolded, splattered in a fine gold dust. A smell of blood. A redness at their feet cemented to the ground. Eight pylons, submerged in a liquid . . . and she rises up out of the thickness and kicks him between the legs where it is soft, red splashes everywhere, as he sits there quite helpless all strung up in a ragged sheet, and she feels his flesh, that softness, give way. She watches him double up in agony, crying out if he could but for the muzzle. And there's a voice coming up out of deep, calling, her voice, that dear voice, saying, "Stop tickling Kev you can never wait. I'll be with you . . . we'll be with you . . . soon . . ." Nobody sees the other one, the child amongst them, fall, fall into a deep pit, fall and disappear below the surface, knees cut open to the bone, blood in streams through cakes of soil. When she can, she picks at the scab, lifting the raw bits.*

Aching in her chest, Molly held herself with pressed crossed arms. She had listened for her friend's footsteps that afternoon . . . her voice . . . reassurance . . . the heavy breathing . . . while drowning underneath a heavyweight. Now, her body weak, she was lying so still she gave the impression of being laid out for burial.

Above her bed on the windowsill the bottles of water caught the light of the late afternoon. She'd collected the water from the ocean and had always intended to give one to Marj.

When she awoke they were the first thing she saw. The light trickled through the glass so that a shadow fell at an angle, wobbly, disturbed, although strangely the water was quite still. She'd been in bed all day: perhaps Marj had been looking for her.

She had to see her friend. But she dreaded that moment.

All Molly was aware of, lying there, alone, was a great gaping space. And because things would never be the same, tears dropped and soaked her pillow.

a life cycle

FOR HER Grade Ten project, Sarah hatched a swarm of big blowflies. They were easier to handle than houseflies. The books say it should take six or seven days for the eggs to emerge, first into larvae, then pupae, and finally develop into adult flies. Sarah's hatching took weeks, with numerous casualties.

"Stick to silkworms and mulberry leaves, Saz," Kate said.

"Oh, but I like flies."

"Butterflies?"

"No, flies."

Eventually she won first prize at the Brisbane Ekka, in a special section for country school exhibitors. A royal-blue ribbon is now draped across a square board of carefully drawn diagrams of all the different stages of the fly's life. Included are examples of a sac of minuscule eggs, a larva's dried-out body, a pupal skin, and an adult fly turned upside down with its legs curled around the body and wings pinned flat. A chicken carcass preserved in its original hatching state lies in an empty fish tank. It looks a surreal object. Molly helped Sarah coat the carcass with a fibreglass resin. It had been eaten out to the centre by the maggots, and hung for weeks by a string under the house, alongside a ripening bunch of lady-finger bananas. It twirled freely as it dried. The two of them transformed the remarkable life story into a work of art. The judges said they were extremely impressed with the exhibit. Molly had even written to Jimmy about it for she thought he might enjoy the artistic blend of scientific detail. He'd been good at that kind of coupling too. And the cyclic way of thinking embodied in the life cycle had a magnetism all of its own. Sarah's coated carcass swings in Molly's mind. From behind as it catches the light it looks like a bronze-cast angel floating on wings.

It would be easy to argue that the past is long dead and better left in that state. Yet how rich a source of knowledge it can be, a blend of fact and fiction, of memory and imagination. As with the maggots in the carcass, you can feed off the past. You can strip it to the bone in order to sup on the marrow, the soft, fatty tissue hidden in the cavity. Molly fed. She found it irresistible, compelling. Just as flies swarmed a carcass, sporing eggs, she began to burrow deeper, eating the tricky bits, nibbling into the centre, the heart.

Before her daughter's project, she knew only that flies hated being interrupted in anything they do. *She* hates being interrupted, having to leave the marrow for another day, for a time when the children are safe at school. She is waiting for the miracle of metamorphosis. Isn't that the reason for going south, to see her friend again? And wasn't it Marj who told her about that, without the fancy name? About the change from an egg to an imago? But who was transforming whom?

invisible mending

AND THEN an awful thought too terrible for words begins to form in Molly's mind, spreads and takes hold. At first not so much a thought as a feeling, a kind of reckoning, a presence of something different, a stranger in her midst. She wants to tell it to go away and leave her. Yet once there, from where she can't tell, it locks into position, refusing to budge. And the words describing the thought, the feeling, the stranger, come to her gradually, in the same stealthy and unnerving way. Her memory becomes dislodged, untrustworthy, as the disconcerting thought threads its way into the contemplative part of her mind. It is so disturbing that she considers turning the Chrysler around to head back home. Right there on the Putty Way, along a piece of road being mended, as the car jolts and bumps over the dirt and potted bitumen. Who would stop her? No one knows she is coming. The girls have never objected to a change of plan before.

Supposing, all along—for this was what her mind was rejecting even as her lips gave shape to the words—just supposing Marj knew, really knew, about Kevin and about her. And, could it be that she knew, not just from after it happened, but from before? Too horrible, opening up a maggot's nest in her mind: that she, Marj, wanted it to happen, gave it authority. And supposing—the words slither about her ungrateful mouth—just supposing Marj participated in that union . . . for her own pleasure! Oh God no!! Impossible. And yet . . . on the day Molly saw her again, the first day since Kevin *fixed her up*, everything Marj talked about beneath the whirring clothesline pointed to that direction, to knowledge, surely.

Marj had called out across the fence as she hung out a load of wet washing. "Molly Rose!" Her voice mingled with fresh grass clippings, damp with a night's dew, and her cotton skirt hitched up under the sides of her cream panties in two hoops, exposed bare dimpled legs. Although it was a voice and a sight Molly had longed for, her full name on Marj's lips threw her.

"You don't mind me calling you Molly *Rose* do you? The Rose part is pretty. Is that what he calls you too? It's sweet . . . Mothers always name children, unless it's a firstborn boy. I saw it on a postcard from your mother, came into my box by mistake. I've told Kev too."

Molly's figure appeared at the back doorstep, in time, in a black beaded cardigan over a cotton dress which hung down to a bandaged ankle. Although she'd been impatient to see Marj, she hesitated now, unsure of what to say. She held a basket of clothes washed many times to rid the fibres of a sourness. She held it in her arms up high across sore breasts. There was a hint of nervousness in her soft round face: she had read the postcard too . . .

Molly Rose,
You love me, you'll come back,
you won't be gone long. Mummy

"Hey, did you hear me?" Marj shouted with *that* voice. "We're late with the washing you know. Should have been

152

out an hour ago, and I've got Barb coming over this morning to taste some cakes and I haven't seen you for ages. What have you been doing with yourself? Kevin told me you'd had an accident and he fixed you up. He's a good man. Is your foot all right now? There's a heart in there, I know it, big and juicy. It's just that sometimes I can't hear it ticking!"

Kevin was at work. Molly had heard him bang the front fly door, stomp across the cement porch and roll down the path, brushing sprays of flowers with his navy overalls, an undersized lunch box hanging from his short fat arm. It was in the shape of a suitcase, only tiny, box brown with silver metal studs, swinging limply, packed by Marj, so strangely out of proportion with his body. A cigarette hung from his mouth. He looked ill-fitting and absurd, especially against the line of young gums crowded with delicate flowers and foraging honeyeaters and bees, the reborn sky pink and lilac as he swaggered down the middle of the street past Molly's house without a glance. She bit her lip behind the opened slat of the venetian blind.

"Ah, there you are, good girl, getting the washing out before lunch," Marj was chatting on. "It'll be a hot one today, before a change comes again. It's about every six or seven days at the moment. Can't you feel it already? Between me and you, it makes my fat boil." She chortled. Her line was heavy with blue and near-white clothes. Eight pairs of overalls—full-length and bib'n' brace. Ten blue Bonds singlets, stretched and faded. Half a dozen baggy shorts with elastic across their backs. And yellow-stained man-sized underpants with blue stripes around the waistline. "You'd think I never washed!"

The warm morning air blew around Molly's legs and up under her dress as she hung out her washing. She'd placed her basket of wet clothes next to the mound of dug-up soil from Jimmy's pit, so that each time she bent to pick out an item of clothing, she stared at the hole, wondering if she had the strength to fill it in. What with that, and a skirt of newly-planted Black-eyed Susans swirling in a circle at the foot of the line, she felt dizzy and faint.

"A good drying day, that's what I say Molly (I should say Molly *Rose*, I'll never get used to it): stiff and sweet-smelling clothes by lunchtime as I've told you before. Late summer is so stable." Marj paused for a breath. "Mind you, it's like anything—it's both a blessing and a curse. Ah well, it's the beginning of another week and thank God Kev's got work for the next month or so, he's gone in today to sign on, out of my hair. A flick and a whip, that's it." Marj glanced side-ways, then came and rested her arms along the wooden support of the fence, watching the younger woman, steadily.

"Tonight, he'll be gone. Same job, same contractors, drilling holes, tractor work. You'd think he'd get sick of doing it, standing around most of the time, but at least they pay. He'll sleep out under the stars, filthy and stinking. Out there, he'll wear the same clothes for days and come home smelling as rich as off meat, like your Jimmy." Marj waved her arms about pointing in the direction of an imaginary highway. "Always these blue workman's clothes. Even on his days off. Blue. Blue. Bloody blue." She paused again, swatting a blowie near her eye, with a spare hand. "He never leaves the jackhammer alone, you know. It's him all over. Throws his weight behind it. Right from the beginning, it was like that from the day he brought it home. He's deaf from it. And he gets the shakes when he wants to say some-thing, you know, like his tool. He thinks I don't know any-thing, that I'm blind, but I'm not Molly. I see things."

Aware of Marj's watching, penetrating eyes, Molly pegged up her last piece of washing. She squinted into the sun, while her arms stretched and ached to the line's wire.

"That's a nice bra," Marj mused affectionately, jumping all over the place in the conversation like a butterfly searching for nectar. "Nice and lacy, not the twin peaks of the new look. Softer. I used to wear them once, in my younger days. Not quite so daring though, no lace, no wires. Doesn't it cut in?"

Molly looked perturbed, dropped her arms.

"Kev'll look good in a suit, with a flower in the button-hole don't you think? I'll be proud of him then. Do you know Barb's ordered orchids especially? To go with the lily-of-the-valley. They're my favourite too. Cooktown orchids, like the ones on Jimmy's postcard—Queensland's emblem . . ."

She couldn't face Marj, not now, front on, to chat about orchids of all things. Those tattooed onto Kev's chest spread their ink in her mind. She longed to blot them out. In defence, she continued to stare at her clothes, high and drying. A couple of bras, seamed stockings, new frilly nylon pants and full and half slips swirled in a circle, as well as one dress, a favourite.

". . . I guess I could put a few on the cake . . ." Marj pressed on.

That dress—the red favourite—had an open neckline with a tight bodice. It was pleated from the waist and printed with a strip of red and black and bottle-green flowers around the hem. The thin belt had an elongated buckle stitched in the same material to match. Molly loved wearing it.

". . . I've got a trick where you brush flowers with a beaten eggwhite, you don't beat it too hard, sprinkle with castor sugar and allow them to dry out at room temperature. Rose petals are best but I don't have any in flower at present, you know the deep red ones—but I could do the same with an orchid . . ."

It was her going-away outfit and she did more for *that* dress than for the wedding ceremony itself, making it just before leaving for Australia, with Joyce supervising every stitch in her irritating way, thinking there wouldn't be enough time to do it with all the other preparations. But Molly had been determined. There was a short square jacket to match, and, with a single string of imitation ruby beads hanging in a long loop down to the waist, the picture was complete.

". . . You can eat flowers you know," Marj kept on talking, "Geraniums, nasturtiums, all kinds of roses and I'm sure I heard somewhere you could eat orchids as well. Quite good for you, especially tasty coated in sugar. Very decorative."

Orchids and roses. Orchids and roses. The flowers grew in Molly's mind, multiplying rapidly in the heat. Trying to block Marj's incessant talk of edible flowers, she stared at the favourite dress hanging upside down on the line, trying to comfort herself with the familiar lines and contours. Concentrating on her dressmaking and the clothes she loved wearing should soothe her.

"Very decorative, if you treat them delicately. They bruise easily you see. I like that dress—the one you're fingering. You're so thin and elegant in it. It suits you with your hair. Has anyone ever said that?"

No Marj, she wanted to say, never. Her mother thought the buttoned bodice was too tight, accentuating her breasts unnecessarily, the hemline too short and the job too rushed. And Jimmy, well he didn't take any notice the day she wore it, underneath a winter coat, as they waved goodbye at Waterloo Station. He was more concerned with the creases in his cotton suit and the way his polka-dot tie fell down his chest. Despite the cold October sky, they'd both worn their Australian summer clothes.

"It's got a nice line. I can't even *think* of that sort of thing —I'm too big. But it's nice to dream and watch you wear it."

Molly fingered one of the small red buttons and her mending underneath it. Her chest ached.

"Funny, 'cause Kev always liked me in red. What are you looking at, has it torn?"

"It's nothing." Molly didn't let on that it had broken off the day she sprained her ankle—the day Kev *fixed her up*— that it was more than nothing. She had patched the bodice carefully, with her machine and by hand: tacking the thread across the frayed L-shape tear, cutting a square from the generous hem, reinforcing the back with the extra material and folding the raw edges under, then sewing on the red button again with pin-sized stitches. Her needle had gone in and up and through the two holes, then down, again and again, making the button secure. Before finishing off, she'd wound the cotton thread around in a circle, between the material and button. Joyce had warned her it was important to mend well so as to completely hide any damage; look as good as new; forget there was ever a tear or a hole or a mishap; and cover a mistake in judgment. Her mother would be proud of the invisible mending.

"I've got a stack of mending to do myself, I'd better get into it sometime, while Kev's occupied."

The red dress flicked into the air, eclipsing the blue sky with a bouquet of flowers. Molly realized she would have to wear her confusion in the fabric of that dress. She'd never be able to shed that skin. In a way she didn't want to. A telling tale. And it was at this point of resignation, as Molly watched the dress float higher, its dampness quickly evaporating in the morning heat, making it as light and airy as a kite, that Marj with a nimble touch brought her back to earth, allaying her fears.

Marj had a deft touch.

She said, "Come and have a cup of tea, you look like you need it. I've just put the kettle on."

In one easy stroke, Marj restored the equilibrium.

Everything seemed to be quite normal.

A hush fell over the houses.

But afraid to trust it, Molly heard herself saying, "Look Marj, not today . . ." Her refusal was limp, in a whisper. She was thinking of Marj's kitchen, the disarray that day, the cold cups of tea with brown stains, the red meat safe with the crawling flies and her aching body now safely wrapped in clothes. She could still smell Kevin . . .

"Aw, come on," Marj said. "We'll be alone, cheer one another up. A nice good strong cup of tea on a hot day never did anyone any harm. Keep company, while the fellas are off. You must be lonely." Marj's plea for normality couldn't have been more potent. Still Molly resisted, distracted, thinking, weren't they now related, strung together by a man?

"That's better," Marj was saying, having a keen eye for the change in Molly's face. "You look like you need it with all those clothes on." She turned to go inside. "You must be hot!"

The gate squeaked as Molly pushed it open into Marj's garden. There was time to change her mind as she paused outside the house, trailing her fingers through the slimy waters of the bird-bath. She could hear Marj singing in the kitchen, almost see her lips in their exaggerated, loose way forming the words as she fussed about, clinking the china. The spiritual's words floated on the warm morning air . . .

Where the ri - ver oh the sweet ri-ver flows Where the
ri - ver the sweet sweet ri-ver flows Come
home come home wash me clean Where the
ri - ver oh the sweet ri-ver flows.

. . . the favourite song, an anthem.

She could quickly make up some excuse; that she had cleaning or sweeping to do; that she was finishing the beading on the veil and the shoes; Barbara's wedding was close and she had no time to waste. But something drove her to be near Marj, to put to rest the suspicion of complicity. To know she *did* please her.

"Come on Molly, you look tired." Marj filled the door-way, her hands on her hips. "That's it." She guided the younger woman into the kitchen, an arm wrapped around her giving support, and gently swayed and pulled the thin shoulders into her cushion breasts and the pocket of her underarms.

"Now we're right. You're good to hold and we're on our own!" she said, their heads interlocking in a full tuck.

If Molly could just hold onto that moment and spread it into eternity, as she would spread a jar of Marj's loquat jam thickly on toast. And ignore the drag of the knife.

Oh sure, the morning tea was relaxed, and Marj invited her for supper. She had said, "Molly, let's have roast lamb tonight decorated with beetroot roses. The men are away and the girls'll keep each other company. I've got a leg and a flap. We'll season it, make some fresh mint sauce for flavour and finish off with this left-over sponge filled with cream and jelly cubes. What do you say to that?" Molly didn't have to say anything about her ankle or Kevin or the stray lemon. She just let Marj talk, and her own tangled thoughts drift.

They'd stirred their hot tea with silver souvenir spoons, Molly in an even circle, steadying her hand, wanting something to do, mesmerized by Marj's chatter. But then Marj began to dig around, disturbing the surface. She said, "Molly, you're shivering."

"I'm all right."

"You don't look all right. You're really shivering, even on a hot day. What's up?"

"No truly . . ."

"I've been talking too long and too hard . . . is that it? I'm sorry. I really am."

"Marj . . ."

"Something's happened? It's Jimmy isn't it? The postcard. You're worried?"

"Marj . . ."

"It is Jimmy's postcard. Maybe it's all a mistake, you misread him, he'll change his mind and not go."

"No."

"No, you're right, but there's no good worrying over it. You can't do anything, let's face it . . ." Marj began to laugh. It was disconcerting, Molly not sure if it was with her or at her. Marj laughed and shouted, her throat shuddering, "Don't worry about him, let him go home. GO HOME! If he needs to. You've got everything here! Everything!" Marj's voice released the pressure. Flies lifted from the ceiling and walls and benches in a thin black cloud. The kitchen filled with buzzing. "See, they know. They can sense any competition near them, and they lift off the carcass. They know when to shift their buttocks." She laughed, tears rolling now, holding her stomach. "Well at least *I'm* laughing and I better shut the fly door."

To remain calm, Molly helped herself to a large wedge of apple cake, so light. Marj was on to her second large slice: she placed the food into her mouth carefully, and Molly watched her fingers disappear with the cake to the first knuckle, lips closing, Marj's concentrating eyes sparkling with the effort.

"You wouldn't believe it, but a fox got into our chook pen last night." Marj was serious again. She ate as she spoke, shifting the mouthful of cake from one side of her mouth to the other, licking her lips and fingers clean of icing sugar and apple pulp.

"A fox?"

"Yes, Kevin must have left the door open. This morning I found a chook at my doorstep. Disgusting. Didn't you hear the racket?"

Molly didn't answer, she was thinking of other things. The Waters—childhood sweethearts. More than thirty years of marriage. Fat and comfortable, of which she was now a part. Was it the cut of her red dress—the one Marj said looked elegant—or her new shoes? Was it a mistake to surprise him? She did it for Marj, surely. To keep them happy. For her to belong to the Waters' embrace. She took in a big gulp of air.

"I'd never cook it though," Marj was saying, "Although it's still good meat. I can't stand the sound of Kev's sucking on the bones. (Jesus, I'm glad he's going away.) A disgusting noise. Thank God they left me a dozen eggs, I was counting on them. I'll use all twelve. They were hidden, under the straw, or else the fox would have sucked them dry too. You see, fresh eggs don't smell Molly."

And how *did* they manage to sleep together? Was it a squash? Or did they lie together like a sandwich? Economical without filling.

"And think about the orchids will you? I want to know what you think of the colour. You could add a suggestion of it to the dress of the little girl—a ribbon or something. It'll look nice. Purple and apricot. Go and bring in your clothes now, you've left them too late really, they'll be dry for sure. Get them in before they fade to nothing. And Molly, let's have roast lamb tonight, what do you say?"

Molly left Marj's place spinning.

two scarlet gladioli

THAT AFTERNOON before their shared meal, Molly rode in and out of Civic on a mission. She wanted to show Marj how she felt, or perhaps it was more how she wanted to feel. Molly had decided to measure her affection, thinking if she convinced Marj, then it would be possible to share that conviction with herself. So she hoped.

The florist spun the bunch around in her hand, expertly, adjusting the greenery and tissue paper, just so. Molly had chosen a bunch of mixed exotics from a bucket out the front of the shop and she'd already exchanged them for money when she recognized the form of one of the sprays. In the centre of the bunch were two scarlet gladioli. Being timid, however, Molly couldn't bring herself to ask for a replacement.

Back up the hill, as she split the stems to give the flowers a long life, and rested them in her own bucket of water, Molly peered into one of the opening gladiolus buds, more orange than the one Kevin tore when they first met. In an instant she saw Marj scrambling to rake up the torn fragments strewn over the tablecloth, her urgency, those fingertips working overtime. The skirt around the cup of the gladiolus was frilly, doubled over in places and full. Against her will—if only she could stop herself—Molly peeled the skirt back to see what lay inside, to see what Kevin felt that day, at the beginning. Trembling, green stem in hand, she fingered the thick petal . . . and in the private view, she saw the funnel wasn't empty. Inserting her finger and moving it

162

around, gently, she touched the pollen-bearing parts of the flower. Even as she shuddered with memories, her touch gave her strength.

Nothing was going to spoil the friendship, so she extracted the two telling sprays from the bouquet to keep for herself, not wanting Marj to remember. Besides, they were going to eat roast lamb weren't they? Food can allay a thousand fears, preparing it together, then the taking and the eating without anyone else around. Everything had to be quite normal.

Dressing for tea, Molly felt confident again. This was a necessity, for not only was her friendship with Marj at stake, but Joyce had been writing too. So, perhaps it was simply the look and touch of her clothes that calmed her. On her bed she had laid out one of her best dresses, *haute couture*, a green spotted rayon number lined with silk, with a kick pleat at the back. She felt a part of the Parisian catwalk with it on: it fitted the line of the body closely, her bare white shoulders highlighted the shaped bodice and a pleated flounce looped across the neckline. Touching any silky fabric had soothed and comforted her always. Not only did caressing those surfaces make her feel at home with herself, it sparked off a run of something profound and quite sensual. Beside the green dress, the colour of jade, she lay out her underclothes, suspenders, a pair of silk stockings, her repaired shoes, and at the end of the row, ready to slip under the pillow, a pile of Joyce's letters.

She'd written, *Rosy, I could tell that something was wrong that you'd really gone. All day I sat in my chair. I couldn't move my legs slept a little I suppose on and off like a blinking light or the moon shining then disappearing behind clouds. I sat there all day it might have been a couple of days for all I know with a knitted rug made out of coloured scraps hanging over the side limp and loose but well-protected and still completely still.*

Entering through the back door with the bouquet of flowers over her arm minus the telltale gladioli, Molly sensed victory, if only for a night. Between her breasts she'd clipped a large brooch to hold the low neckline together. The purple stone shone against the jade rayon and her white velvet shoulders in a rich counterpoise. Snatching a good look in the mirror, she felt like a beautiful peacock. Marj whistled with delight. She loved the bouquet too, and took her time setting them in a vase with sugar and bleach, humming snatches of her song, *Where the river oh the sweet river flows*, clipping and poking the stems into a half dome of green glass holes, the flowers evenly spaced and well-supported. The dome filled the neck of a tall patterned vase, clinking into position. Before eating, Marj placed the flowers in the centre of her table laid for her roast.

Back home, near midnight, the confidence Molly had felt ebbed away. Unable to sleep, she read more of her mother's letters, then buried them in Jimmy's pit. Joyce was leading her somewhere, somewhere dark.

   . . . I sat there all day Rosy in my chair. I didn't care about the seeping puddles a warm wetness sodden cushion sitting astride the boggy marsh I grew up in but it wasn't cold for my body warmed the spot. I remember details well don't you think? They must have been banging for a time. I heard a twist of the key in the lock. Mrs Chamberlin remembered where it was tucked up between the bricks at the back door those brown bricks I do love. Knocking. Silence. The sun cast shadows over the ground. Then a key in a hole harder fitting perfectly metal against metal. Joyce Joyce where are you? We were worried terribly worried I've brought some nice men to help men from the hospital. Their shouting made my head ache. I searched for another cloud the privacy of a cloud but I wish you were here Rosy to hide me with dark furry wings. All I've been trained to do is to go home, back to the cracked knobbly hands . . .

   Joyce loved her birds, her pigeons, they were part of the family. Molly did too in a funny sort of way, in the way you grew used to things, fond of things you lived with. It was her grandfather who taught her how to look after them. She remembered him well; his bushy eyebrows and the way he'd scowl at her in a teasing mood, his rough unshaven cheek with its musty smell and the way he'd clear his throat with punctuating uh-hem noises that made her want to bang his back. He'd take Molly out the back of the house, holding her small hand in his, to see the pigeons in their cages. He showed her how to feed the birds and clear out the cage, how to set them free and count them on return.

. . . I was so comfortable looking out from my cave sitting in warm water remembering him, Joyce's voice in Molly's head grew louder, *his cracked knobbly hands reaching in to unhook the latch of the cage and the pigeons fluffing and rustling with excitement. I can see him from the other side through the coop's hexagonal holes. Dad sang love songs on and on—he was singing to me too—as if he'd never be able to lift the latch and let them go. I'd jump up and down yelping at first then stronger, shouting at Dad, Let them out! Let them out! I hated them being all cooped up. And he'd yell back at me to shout louder and I would, him winding me up with More, more, Joycey girl, my father smothering me, me shouting for release, until we collapsed in each other's arms with the pigeons in a flurry over our heads . . .*

Molly waited for weeks until she knew the gladioli were quite dead, before burying them in the garden along with the latest of her mother's letters, for she grew afraid of reading them.

Outside, there was just enough light from a small moon to see what she was doing. She threw the galdioli into Jimmy's pit before shredding the bundle of letters into long strips. Then she sat on the mound beside the hole, her knees tucked under her chin with one arm supporting them, the other hand fiddling with fistfuls of earth. She thought of Jimmy, and the way he kneaded clods of soil like knobs of pastry, feeling the texture with his large fingers. She imagined him there, teaching her how to do it, her muscles working harder and harder, the clay softening. She remembered Jimmy proudly holding up the bracelets he'd made out of the clay so she could admire them from the kitchen window. She tried making one now, in the darkness, stiff with cold. But the circles she fashioned out of long thin rods cracked and fell apart.

She let the soil finish the process of decomposition, turning her flowers and the onion-skinned paper into fresh compost. Black gold.

a nest of eggs

MOLLY WOULD have liked to have stopped there, paused a little. She sensed things were changing but not in the way she'd imagined. The two women had a lot to do, for the wedding was close; and they could concentrate on practical matters. Marj of course, was adept at this, although she wasn't afraid to ask Molly's advice.

Marj said, "Do you think a few chocolate and candy eggs would look good in amongst the sweet plates?"

"Well it *is* an Easter wedding. Easter Saturday," Molly replied.

"Not overdoing it?"

"I've got some scraps of tulle to make a nest. You could make a nest in a basket, lay the eggs in it and decorate the handle with ribbon and bows. I think it'd look nice," Molly said with authority.

Molly kept writing to her mother about the details of the wedding, not knowing what else to do. She wrote, *February, Dear Mummy, Everything is nearly ready, the flower girl will look quite sweet, tight fitting, but that's what Barbara wanted. I'm helping Marj with the food . . .*

"I could do a few fakes as well for the nest," Marj suggested, "Blown eggs. As kids we'd prick the ends with a pin and blow, hard, our cheeks puffed out like pumpkins— Beaudesert Blues. The eggwhite and yolk slithered out— slimy and wet and running together—squeezed through the pinhole. You'd think you'd never do it, that your cheeks would crack first. But it works. You should try it. I love decorated eggs with paint and dye."

. . . I'd like to go north on the money I'll make. Marj says she'll take me there and show me everything . . .

Then one day, Molly slumped with a weight that only knowledge can deliver. If she were to name it, she felt a sadness. Sad because some things were changing while others remained the same, because it was all so unfair. Sad because of the way people became caught up in other lives and circumstances over which they had little control. First Marj and then Joyce put an end to the finely tuned see-saw she was balanced on.

It happened the day Marj took Molly's hand and led her, a little reluctantly at first, through the hallway to the master bedroom. Did Marj sense her hesitation? The family portrait smiled. But there alongside the double bed lay a camp bed, both beds made up and ready for sleeping. Holding hands with Marj, especially in that room, Molly felt close, although she could feel Kevin's fingers curl around her own thin ones. Thick with Marj, she was a joint partner to his body.

"Kevin likes to hold my hand in the night," Marj began.

Not all the time then? Only once in a while? Molly remembered the mattress curving into a hollow, and his body over hers in a reluctant stain of heat. Was she an easy sex-aid for a marriage that had lost its fire? But she was determined to be faithful to Marj.

As if to confirm it though, Marj added, "We sleep separately sometimes. But I want to show you something Molly." Without a pause, Marj raced on about other things, as if to quell lurking suspicions. "Here, in my special drawer—my favourite toy, kept all these years. It's an egg from a Queensland rainforest—red cedar. If I'm anxious at all then this egg comforts me, it's the same as cooking a sponge, it's something women can do. There was an old woman living behind us, everyone else thought she was a witch but I didn't. I went there after school and talked. Her house smelt musty and we had endless cups of tea and orange cakes. Her hands shook as she served the tea and there were always cake forks and serviettes—she was a proper lady you see. Then she died. I found her—spread out on the floor near the back door, not a mark, no struggle. Afternoon tea was all ready that day, set for two, for her and me, and in the cake tin there was a small parcel wrapped in old Christmas paper— to Marjy (that's what she called me). My hands trembled when I opened it, I remember the wobble. She gave me this, from her home."

Through the veil of sadness, Marj gave Molly a large wooden egg, its polished red skin smooth and cold to touch like a real one.

"Open it, unscrew it, there are more inside. They lie like that, one inside the other, till you can't go any further. As smooth as a baby's bottom."

Molly laid out the nest of eggs on the bed. Six eggs, from the largest to the smallest in diminishing sizes.

"I tried to eat it!" Marj laughed, pointing to the tiny one, solid wood and stained more brown than red. "Cracked my tooth I did!"

Molly smiled. She held the tiny one in the cup of her hand.

"They bulldozed Gracie's house. I came home from school one day and it was all gone, everything, right down to the plumbing. Since then I've had to imagine what it was like."

Late in the afternoon, and on the same day that Molly had listened to Marj's story while cradling the interlocking eggs and warming their smooth skins, she opened another of Joyce's letters with a knife.

Dear Rosy, her mother had written at the top of a blank page in her distinctive handwriting. Unwrapping the fine sheet of onion-skin paper, Molly pulled out an old photograph. Its edges were ragged as if the image had been cut out of a larger family group shot. The photograph was yellow with age, the surface dappled. It must have been taken before

Molly was born, she was sure of it, and as she stared at it she had the impression she'd seen it before. This couldn't be right as she never remembered looking at photos, so she dismissed the thought. And yet, and yet, a familiarity haunted her.

The photograph was of a young woman, a handsome woman, with a head of lush and beautiful hair. There was no smile on her face but the eyes, framed by the startling eyebrows like two exotic and generous wings, caught the onlooker's gaze. They came at you even from out of the depths of the image, despite the distraction of her beauty. They locked the observer into a dreaming world, a world where the unthinkable was possible. And although there were many pointers to the subject's identity, the wealth of hair and the way the woman leant against the rock, it was those eyes more than anything else, that Molly recognized in a flash. Her heart tightened and her throat hurt as she gazed at the image. The woman was none other than her mother, Joyce Moone née Bridges, young and beautiful and round with child.

Why did Joyce send this? Now?

The haunting eyes stared at Molly, begging for a response, for love, affection, while punishing her at the same time. Molly knew she'd never be able to tell her mother what had happened to her, about Kevin, about her body changing. Afraid, Molly took the photo to the bathroom and with a sharp pair of scissors cut up the image, those eyes, into a hundred pieces and flushed them down the toilet. The sudden rush of water drowned the conflicting voices in her head.

With relief, she lay across the covers on her bed thinking back to the rest of the day, to Marj and the story of the witch called Gracie who'd lived behind her, and to the eggs with their interlocking patterns. To calm herself, she imagined unscrewing the eggs and arranging them in a neat line. If she could, she'd like to hold the smallest in the cup of her hand again and feel its smooth polished skin.

red lipstick

JIMMY CAME home in a terrible state. He turned up at the front door close to the end of eight weeks and it was as if he came back into focus suddenly, Molly having to reach out to him from a dream. She wasn't prepared.

She heaved one of his bags and swag down the hall wishing she'd a little more time, wondering what to say to him, hoping he wouldn't ask questions about the time apart. They were uncomfortable with each other, Molly impatient for the next move.

Thinking back on that day, all she remembers were his large feet in brown lace-ups as she opened the door, his looming presence, and the sound of his heavy step following her down the hall. Molly must have said something kind to him when they came to his room to put down the luggage, for she also remembers he smiled at her. Did she smile back?

Over the years she'd kept all his correspondence in two matching hatboxes for safekeeping. She tied the bundles with rafia ribbon. He wrote in jerks or spasms, where, after a long period of not hearing from him, he flooded her with words. She saved the letters unopened till long after the twins were in bed. She felt the thickness of paper folded neatly into the blue square airmail envelope with her name— Ms Molly Moone at her specific request and uncontested by him— written in small tight copybook letters on the front. His handwriting was as neat and precise as the way he dressed, and his letters were good to read. They were thoughtful, well-rounded, educated, littered with quotes from texts and scientific manuals, the biographies and novels he was reading. He never stuttered on the page. In return, Molly scrawled off letters and postcards with ease, telling him about her moves, and often referring to the south-east corner of Queensland she lived in, the Wallum country, excited a little by the attachment they were creating through this mutual interest in the descriptive world of soils. Both felt comfortable talking about the earth under their feet, the famous giant coastal podsols of the Sunshine Coast they learnt about, and the difficulties arising from the rapid but uneasy intrusion of short-sighted urban development. It gave them something firm to stick to, and Molly was surprised at her growing understanding. They worked well together: Jimmy, from a safe, learned distance; Molly from an immediate, anti-development stance.

Their letters were rarely personal, however, neither confessing to the other the importance of the fabric being woven between them. The nature of their relationship remained hidden and elusive, unvoiced.

And then one day a letter arrived, after a little silence, which did nothing to alert Molly for it was quite within the bounds of their long-distance conversation. Yet in one move it altered the rules forever. It had been an ordinary day. She'd come home from work to the flat, collected the girls from a friend's place, dumped her basket on the circular kitchen table, pulled off her straw hat with the black scarf draped around it and had gone back out the front door to the letterbox to collect the mail before cooking tea. There, amongst a bundle of bills and junk mail, was an aerogram with its Royal Mail insignia in red and blue. At first she thought there was some mistake, for the only overseas letters she received were Jimmy's, in regulation square envelopes, in blue, tan or pink. But the familiar handwritten letters, small and neat, jabbed at her.

In the same way years before, when Jimmy had come home at the end of eight weeks in the field in Western

Queensland, his voice in its thin and rasping way jabbed at her.

"R–Rosy," he'd called out from the garden, "I'm c–coming in now." At her name being called she felt a warmth creeping up the back of her neck, a shock of adrenalin through her body. She clung to him then, strangely torn with desire, wanting to lie with him.

Jimmy hadn't been home long, but before he even had time to shower, Kevin called in to have a drink. He had a bag of bottles with him. Molly made herself scarce when she heard him knock and call out at the door, but Jimmy obliged, perhaps caught out by courtesy, or more likely disarmed. After six months in Australia, his colours had run and faded with the elements. He didn't even bother with top pocket handkerchiefs any more. It was all too harsh. He'd have a drink with Kev; he'd learnt how to do it while up north.

From the kitchen window, Molly watched the men take the bottles outside and stand around Jimmy's pit, a drink in hand. She wondered if Jimmy noticed the hole had been filled in a little so that the bottom wasn't flat and hard as he preferred, but uneven and soft with turned soil, and the old shovel she'd used to do it was still there, leaning against one side. In the growing darkness she observed the shadowy figures, Kevin laughing, his fat vibrating uncontrollably, those eyes disappearing for sure, and Jimmy bending down close to the ground, his arms spread out wide, shielding his hole from mockery. Would he begin to dig again, now that he was back? She hoped Joyce's shredded letters and the gladioli were decomposing fast.

When he came in much later, she knew he was drunk; he smelt of beer and freshly turned soil. His stammer was worse with alcohol, his tongue slipping around his open mouth like an eel. He said: "I've heard the ssss–strangest thing t–tt–tonight. K–K–K, you know, K–Kevin t–t–old me . . ."

"Told you what?" Her voice had an edge to it. She felt herself slip and slide a little.

"Told me he'd sss—seen you. He w—wwwwwhispered it into my ear." Jimmy slurred his words with a smile of pleasure, as he stumbled towards his bedroom.

"Seen me?"

"Your lll—legs." He garbled, hardly audible, suffocating the words with his feather pillow he'd pulled out of the swag. Its slip was grey and thin with wear. His black stringy hair flopped. He said: "I've been th—thinking," and he paused, just long enough for Molly to detect a change in his eyes, a hardening, as if he'd made up his mind about something. "We'll ggg—g—go next month Molly. I'll arrange our pppp—passage." He talked to the pillow, alone with the woman in his arms. "It'ssss almost . . . sss—six months."

Molly broke into a sweat. "I'm not going with you." She sank her teeth into the words, sounding them out, deliberating.

"Your mother will be pleased, she needs you . . ."

"I'm not going home. I'm staying here."

"You ggg—gg—ggo where I ggg—go Rosy."

"I'm not going back to England."

She stood beside the bed, her arms crossed for support, gazing at his hands dirty with soil. "I don't have to, I want to make a go of it here," she said quietly. He wasn't gripping her as he used to, he'd changed. In her mouth she could taste something fresh—the first sweetness for a long time. And although there were many unanswered questions, her voice must have soothed Jimmy for he nodded in agreement as she suggested, "Let's talk about it in the morning Jimmy, you need your sleep now."

She tucked him into the bed, sliding his heavy legs covered with infected sores under the covers (she'd have to get onto them before he left), and planted a big kiss on his forehead. Her lips left a clear red lipstick mark.

In Molly's memory, the seal on Jimmy's forehead glows like a brand in the dark. She sees it from afar: her red lips on his forehead. Would she recognize him when he visited? Marked forever with a kiss. In the aerogram, he told her he still loved her. She unfurls the words in her mind, touches with a fingertip the drying boronia she'd kept as a promise.

He wrote: *When I think back to when I left you, my overwhelming feeling is shame. I shouldn't have done it, left you alone like that I mean, and I want to do something about it . . . Now, what I want to tell you is that I have a little money in store. I've been paid out early with a handsome golden handshake and I want to do something worthwhile with it, I want to come back to Australia to visit, nothing heavy of course, just to see you. I know you've got your own life with your girls, and I would never insist on a closeness, but I just thought we could see each other again.*

Molly remembers Marj saying, If you wait long enough love, you'll get fed in the end. There was little doubt Jimmy had remained faithful to her, even if at arm's length. Could she trust him further? He'd been good to Joyce too. It broke Molly's heart remembering her mother, for back then, any confidence she might have felt had been undermined. Her memory traces the lines of her mother's face in the photo she'd destroyed, her beauty, and it makes Molly think of Jimmy trying to find his mother on the streets and in buses, everywhere, and him telling her this while stroking the piece of driftwood which lay as decoration in the middle of the table they shared at Bawley Point.

He wrote: *It's been a long time Rosy, and you mean a lot to me. You see I still love you, like I did back then. I love Australia* too. I've been reading D. H. Lawrence's *Kangaroo* where he writes, "I want Australia." He understands, as I hope you do. "I want Australia like a man wants a woman. I fairly tremble with wanting it." Tell me that you'll see me again. It won't be heavy, promise. Let me know soon.

homing pigeons

THE FAT fingers moved across the garden in a whisper, as if they were in love. The fat fingers tickled and teased the seedlings, skirting around the plants in arcs and spirals, brushing the foliage. They prodded and poked at weeds. They twisted the splayed heads carefully at the base and pulled the roots, letting the good plants breathe, the ones that remained bear fruit.

To create some kind of order, Molly began to spy on Marj. It was a way of staying calm. It was a way of stalling.

There was the time she watched Marj garden from the other side of the fence, in secret, at twilight. Molly watched her weeding out the rubbish. Moving in slow motion, bewitched by a garden in half-light, Molly was intoxicated with her friend's fingers, their dexterity, capabilities and touch.

Spying made Molly a little hot.

Once when she did this, Marj had shouted at her as if she knew eyes were watching her, "It's going to be hot today, why have you got all those clothes on?" On this occasion, it was morning, the washing was out. Marj said: "Hot here means hot love. It might be nearly autumn, but the sun's still warm. You've got to keep cool."

Molly was watching Marj transplant seedlings from a tray into finger-sized holes in the damp brown earth. She wore man-size gloves for protection and pressed the soil around the plant. Hard and firm. Perhaps, Molly was thinking, she'd been a spy since she arrived, forever on the rim.

"What are you planting?" she asked Marj, pulling the cardigan more firmly around her shoulders.

"Daisies. Kevin asked especially for them. He's funny like that. Doesn't do a thing in the garden except mow the lawn now and then into two shades, and I can manage that myself but he insists. But he does sometimes come out with very definite ideas. Says it'd be nice for Barbara—give a bit of floor covering as a border to the draped white tablecloths. They should flower in time, because they're good-sized plants. Don't mind them myself really. In the right place. I'll put them around the bird-bath too.

"And to keep the snails away, I'll put these here." Marj sunk three empty tins into the earth, their rims at ground level, and filled them with frothing amber beer. "Kev will just have to put up with this, if he wants some flowers. The silly buggers smell this stuff, fall into it, get drunk, and never find their way out."

"Jimmy's going home," Molly said. Her voice was flat. It was settled. When Jimmy had talked about it again that morning in the kitchen, she'd scalded her tongue on hot breakfast tea.

"I'll book, Rosy," he'd said, having rehearsed the lines. "I'll go by train, then plane." His face was pale and he shuffled across the kitchen in slippers, with a stoop. He didn't say a word about her.

She stared at him.

And he faltered then, his jaw rigid suddenly, his fingers fiddling with things on the table.

"I can't bear it Jimmy," Molly fairly shouted. "Write it all down, for God's sake, whatever you have to say to me . . . Go on, damn it, don't be ashamed!"

He unclenched his mouth, gripped a chair, released it and lunged at a pen and some paper. He wrote:

I'm going home.
Need a holiday.
Six weeks at least. But

I want you to come with me.

"So he's decided once and for all." Marj said, pulling her big hands out of the canvas gloves.

"He wants me to go and I said no."

It sounded so straightforward to say. Intoxicating the night before, when he was drunk, her teeth biting the words —*I'm not going with you*—she'd tasted something fresh and sweet. But as he stood there the next morning, pen in hand, she'd stumbled, "I can't go," fishing around inside her head for a reason, an excuse, listening to the casuarinas whispering suggestions. On windy days Molly could hear them in the bush at the back. They whistled and shunted in the rustled air, while noisy clouds of sulphur-crested cockatoos cavorted through the branches, cracking seed and carelessly throwing it onto the ground.

"This job isn't finished until the wedding day. Marj wants me there." She kept going, filling the air with words. "The dresses are ready, but they may need adjusting, Barbara may put on weight and I've got the headpieces to do. Damn it Jimmy, this is really important, I can't let Marj down. I couldn't possibly go anywhere. I'll keep house for her, anything, to stay." Her words had accelerated, tripping over each other, and then she stopped, abruptly, saying, "I'll do anything to stay. Truly."

Jimmy turned his back, and wrote:

what will they say
at home?

"Tell them the truth, that my work is important, that you wanted to go home."

Home. Home was her mother: *someone died in the next room at tea time they washed her in a liquid to kill birds what a strong smell I slept on my stomach face buried into my favourite pillow cover and I dreamed I dreamed I made a wreath for Daddy's grave out of tiny roses the thorns scraping and pricking my fingers so that they were covered in beads of fresh blood I dreamed I laid the wreath and a hand sprang out*

179

*of the grave I screamed and it was scratched and bleeding and
raw and I shrieked and shoved it back into the soil and it kept
flying back up again and again and I dug with my hands to
cover the hand the wet earth up my nails and hurting blood
everywhere and my hysteria and the mound a drowning
oversized egg*

Did I tell you that Fudge dropped dead too?

"So you said no," Marj said. She continued to spray the
hose over her new plants, glancing up every now and again
to look at Molly, to reassure her.

"The first time, he didn't hear me," Molly was saying,
giving voice to her wandering thoughts. "Drunk too much,
one glass is enough for him. The second time, I met it front
on, said I wanted to see more of Australia, before I thought
about going home . . . He asked how long that would take,
I said over a year, maybe two. He asked me whether it was
you . . ." Molly tilted her head towards Marj.

"And . . .?"

Molly bit her lip, marking time. "I said . . . yes." And
then, all in a rush because her friend was warm towards her
and she was tired, she said, "I didn't want to go home, I told
him home was here Marj, home was here and he said it was
only a holiday and that he'd be back."

"Do you believe him?"

"Ah . . . I don't know . . . what do I say to Mummy?"
She swallowed hard. "I've got to work out what to write."

*. . . feathers and fluff block out the sun until they fly high
in a bunch around and up and down and around making
patterns and I leave the note scrawled in red ink in my cage
the wooden door swinging the hook banging against the wire
feathers and fluff and a smell of manure and straw my smell
I'm back in time for hot buttered toast marmalade black tea
pigeons always fly home for breakfast . . .*

"Does she need to know?" Marj asked.

"I don't think she'd realize. I'm getting strange letters
from her . . ." Molly tried to sound offhand.

"What if Jimmy visits her?"

. . . I shouted Let them out! Let them out! and Daddy said Come on Joycey! Come on! and at last just as Mother's face showed at the kitchen window wondering what all the commotion was about clearing the fogged glass with the back of her hand just then as they scraped against the wire restless and anxious to get out just then their cooing noise deafening us just then like an act of divine mercy before the pigeons rubbed holes in their breasts just then Daddy would unlatch the hook with a flick of his wrist and sigh and sometimes I wasn't prepared out of time so I didn't hear his tiny pause taking air before he let go. I was too interested in my own part unaware of the following bar of music so I missed the flick just like missing the climax in a piece of music because of an itching knee losing concentration in a flash it is gone and I missed it but they do come back for more—pigeons always fly home for breakfast

A week before Jimmy left, Molly hung out his washing in the morning sunlight to be ready for packing. She stared at his pit and mound of dug-up soil, as if searching for something, a clue to Jimmy's character. That evening she folded pairs of socks, laying the left and right close together, then curling them up in a tight ball, covering one with the other.

"Don't see Mummy, she doesn't have to know," she said to Jimmy in an abrupt way, unsure if she could trust him.

"No." Jimmy drummed his fingers on the bench top. He whistled and fiddled with the laundered clothes.

"You never stick and stay, do you, I guess the money's no problem. Don't undo them Jimmy. I'm not folding those socks again!"

She listened to the pitch of his whistles.

"You b–b–belong here n–now," he said, straightening a collar.

"Yes."

181

The day arrived at last, and as Marj parked the car Molly kissed Jimmy on the forehead between anxious eyes. His bags were loaded on the train and they all waited at the door for a signal from the guard. A heavy overcoat hung over his shoulder.

Molly's lips left a clear red mark as before, a pursed lip-stick kiss, a calculated kiss recognizing their separateness. A kiss she regretted giving, for with it, he lunged at her, greedy for more. Molly's hand shook, clenched down her side.

He asked, "W–w–ill I s–s–see you ag–ag–again?"

"Jimmy, I don't know, the train . . . get in . . ." She waved her hands about as sweat dripped from her underarms and from between her breasts. Her stomach lurched. "You've got to go Jimmy . . ." She stood closer to Marj.

He whistled frantically. "K–k–k–kiss m–me ag–again Rosy?" and his eyes wandered from Molly to Marj, his differently coloured irises in a swirl.

Molly leant forward and kissed him again, hoping with that to rush him through the door. She feared his hesitation and the strength of his gaze.

Her lips left a collage of mixed desire.

It was close to dying: saying goodbye.

They clasped hands as a wave of cockatoos screamed overhead. An eternity passed before Jimmy finally turned. He stepped up off the platform and disappeared. The long snake edged out of the station and the two women walked away silently. Arm in arm, they spent the afternoon strolling through Griffith and Manuka, reciting to one another the biological names of the plants they saw.

Alone and back in her house, Molly felt sad. Easy before in the plan. Easier still, arm in arm with Marj. She comforted herself by thinking of her neighbour in her garden, spying on her in her mind, for she loved the way Marj prodded the sea of leafy salad greens with flapping garden-glove fingers, tickling, teasing, pinching this one and that, before making a final choice. She thinned and weeded all at the one time, murmuring to herself, sometimes humming a tune, her fat awesome buttocks swaying with the movement of the fingers, rocking in time.

ripening skins

IT IS possible to live, I mean to *live*, in the past.

She's thinking. She's dreaming. The obsessed cannot escape.

To *live!*

Don't you think? Marj? You wouldn't disappoint me would you?

As a way of sifting through her thoughts, she sometimes jotted down clues or pointers to her obsession with the past in between medicinal instructions, recipes and shopping lists. The workings of her mind and heart lay hidden in the yellow spiral notebook with a flip-top edge, tucked away in the saltcellar. By writing it down, she was able to spin a skin.

But she was careful never to record the telling details—the taking and the eating. She was silent about the things that happened in the six months in Canberra as a newly-wed and Ten Pounder. She kept *that* on the inside of the skin, out of fear, out of confusion.

Jimmy never knew what happened, the things she hid. He was gone. In a way his leaving had been plain from the beginning, for he never lost his Englishness, his foreignness. He kept his sense of separation close like a favourite coat he couldn't do without. He'd never been *in* Australia, truly a part of the landscape, even though he'd tried. Jimmy loved Australia as an armchair adventurer would, fairly trembling with want, from afar, as an idea, looking into the circle from the safety of the outside rim.

But wasn't that why she had loved him? Together they'd

decided to enjoy the view from the rim, hand in hand? Together they had given their going strength? With mandarins and long white candles and cut flowers from out of Marj's garden Molly decorated her kitchen table. The candles' glow painted the walls and ceiling pale orange. Shadowy ovations. But she felt chilled, empty, forsaken. It was difficult to believe Jimmy was gone from the house, gone from her life. Would he return? Thinking back, she wished she had had the strength to hold his hand more firmly, to reassure him of the possibility of staying. What had changed then? Was it the child embedded in Molly's body that she knew about even as she kissed Jimmy's forehead in farewell? Half of her wanted it for his sake and if it were possible, she'd tell him it was his. Yet this was laughable as she watched him in her mind curl his body to the inside.

Where did that leave her? With the wedding? She would finish off the bridesmaids' lemon organza dresses and the lace on her own ensemble. Hardly enough for an anchor.

And there was Marj, under a big sky, out in the sun and so strong, with runaway wisps of dark hair blowing across her face, brown arms bare and dependable as she pegged out her millionth pair of underpants. Marj said anything that came to mind. Like a public billboard declaring itself in bold black writing, she thought on the outside, plain to see. Couldn't Molly trust her then? What would make Marj break? Did she ever hold her breasts, not being able to bear the throb any longer? Did she ever witness his wary look? Did she *know* him, his jelly weight on top of hers?

Molly watched closely, seduced by her friend's dear form, keenly aware of her own prickling skin, a heat. She would do anything for Marj.

In the middle of the garden, close to the spider-frame rotary hoist, there was the bird-bath carved out of pink stone. Three naked girls held a dish of water with extended arms, effortlessly. Perfect forms, their ankles were crossed with ease. They were quite bald all over, a girl-crack between their legs, dream bodies, sculptured by men no doubt. A frilled collar of newly-planted English daisy seedlings danced at their feet. Molly had seen it before, but not with the same clarity as now. Alone they could do nothing, for the weight would be too much. But together . . .

She watched Marj bend over and pick out a wet white petticoat and stretch to the line, juggling a handful of pegs.

There . . . Molly imagined she felt Marj's strong upturned arms holding the weight of the bird-bath with her—a large Hills-hoist-sized bird-bath. Parrots and lorikeets and crimson rosellas would twirl and pirouette, balancing with three-pronged claws on the bird-bath's fancy perimeter. And Marj's big bare brown arms would rest next to hers, smooth and warm, their fingers touching. Skin brushed lightly, with dark hair between their legs in defiance, large breasts drooping and thick fleshy thighs free from constriction.

Imagine the sculptured girls were women.

Imagine them breaking out of their naked poses.

Imagine them taking things into their own hands, throwing the stone water dish across the garden till it smashed into smithereens, and dancing, after dark.

Imagine them twirling, freely, without shame or fear, naked and hairy, waiting for no one, with only a moon watching.

Molly stood alone, shaking, spying.

go to the river

AN ARM rested across black brush grooves, its elbow in the sun.

If a position or a way of being was able to express a full experience, then it would be that elbow, poking out of the Vanguard, hot with the sun. In that position, Molly felt carefree and wholesome.

She sat beside Marj on the red vinyl bench seat of the Vanguard with all the windows wound down, the wind tangled in her thick loose hair.

Wild daisies lined the open stretch of road, swaying in the strong breeze. The flowering heads were heavy with dozens of yellow and pink faces.

"They're smiling and waving at us Marj." Molly was sensing an opportunity with this outing. It wouldn't be long now before she'd have to tell. Tell all. The signs didn't lie. The question was how to say it? And when? And, how far she trusted her own tongue not to say too much.

"It's a bit late in the season for them," Marj was saying. "We'll go down through Michelago, on the road to Cooma, see the Tinderries on the left of the valley—then turn right to the Murrumbidgee. A bit of a drive, but you'll see some good country and get to the water for lunch. I've made a special tropical spread for our sandwiches." Marj shouted as she hung over the steering wheel, her knees wide apart with a light wool dress pulled up across her thighs.

Molly stroked Marj's shoulder with the tips of her fingers, ever so lightly, one arm extended along the back of the seat, a little nervous. She remembered seeing Marj for the first time, a time full of uncomplicated longing and pleasure, no confusion, when she'd breezed into their kitchen with a prepared supper in a hamper and a vase of dusty wattle for the new neighbours. Was she dreaming, or was it now simple and straightforward, like the beginning? Molly's other hand pressed against the red vinyl bench seat, in a fist. Jimmy was gone and Kevin a mirage in the distance to whom she felt a strange stirring of affection because of his seed in her body, a fragile movement signalling hope. Her eyes filled with tears and spilled over, glistening as they dropped to make two warm wet patches on her legs.

Then she stroked Marj's skin more bluntly, reckless with her tears and the fresh air, her fingers skating across the brownness, all too aware of the distance between them on the seat, of the stretch of her arm and aching muscle, her rudeness and presumption, but wanting to be close, desiring love, believing *they were* partners, joint partners to his body —supportive and close and trusting—wanting to be soaking wet again with Marj in the back garden, just the two of them whirling beneath a wet green sky, before it all changed.

"Sit close," the older woman whispered, her eyes on the road ahead.

Ah . . . It was all she needed, an invitation, to pull across. Lifting her sweaty thighs off the sticking vinyl, Molly relaxed the clenched fist. She wedged Marj's side into her underarm and breast, an arm around the wide shoulders. So close!

The Tinderry Mountains stood out on the left side of the road. Pushing south and in a line parallel to the Brindabellas' smooth ample form on the right, they were jagged and rough. Their pointed, rocky peaks shadowed by a rising sun were wedged into the fat morning sky. The Murrumbidgee River ran between the two ranges, in places its sides steep and woody and crowded with roots drinking deeply from the water. At the crossing the river was shallow and wide. It was full of smooth rounded rocks, washed and worn and pushed downstream in and out of deep pools before being deposited and left to dry out for years on the banks of the meanders.

"Do you miss him?" Marj asked separating the sandwiches.

"Yes. I do."

"You sound surprised."

"I am, Marj," Molly offered. "I am."

They ate their lunch perched on a large rock in a spotlight of sun.

"Yeah, I wish I'd known him better Molly. Men are good around a house although Kevin has been acting strangely of late. Good thing he'll be back a little before Easter because Barbara would never forgive me if he wasn't there and then after the wedding the planning authority are wanting gangs of men to carve out the lake bed. All the old trees have to go, the homesteads, the race-course, the golf course and not forgetting the good soil. They'll make a few islands out of the rubbish. It's a good job, they'll pay him well." She paused.

Molly broke away and walked gingerly over the bare stones with her naked feet.

"Have you heard from him?" Marj shouted, drawing her back to the rock. "Jimmy?"

"No."

"Ah well, you will Molly, you will. He likes you . . . " and for a moment it looked like Marj was lost for words. She quickly regained her composure and said, "We'll go back the way we came Molly. The Tinderries are good in full light."

telling signs

NOT LONG after the picnic on the Murrumbidgee when the two of them had sat close together like lovers on the Vanguard's bench seat, Molly sensed something was wrong, dreadfully wrong. She had begun to bleed. It was unmistakeable: the gusset of her white panties was stained red, a bright crimson, about a spoonful.

Immediately, Molly wanted to burst in on Marj, and confess, not to Kevin's part in it, but telling her it was *Jimmy*, that he'd given her a going-away present. She wanted her friend's comfort too. Marj would believe her for sure, wasn't that how women supported one another, with trust? And Molly would do everything to make her! . . . But something made her hesitate. A warning bell. It was to do with Kevin, the Kevin in Marj.

And she'd been dreaming about him too, his funeral. The church they were in was on the top of a small hill, nestled amongst the dead of the cemetery. It could have been St John the Baptist, in Reid, the one Barbara was to be married in. A pretty church, made out of sandstone and bluestone, empty, apart from Marj and Molly holding hands in the front pew, the tolling bell ringing in their ears. And Molly dreamt she prayed, there, beside Marj's ample figure and in her own private cathedral, the jumbled words pouring out of her in an invisible cloud around her body. Later, in under the pines with the marble gravestones all tipsy because of the roots, Molly watched a wide-bodied coffin descend with jerks into a deep grave. In her dreaming Marj disappeared, while Molly knelt beside the hole throwing bits and pieces, leaves, stones, twigs, weeds, clods of soil—anything she could find—in after him.

After lunch, Molly heard the news of Kevin's return. Marj's loud voice glided over the fence. "He's back." With distance between Molly and Kevin, anything was possible, but in close proximity, she lost heart. Having his bold figure in plain view again, tucked in close, next door, her courage failed her. Not that she thought he'd have told Marj: no, men weren't like that. It was more his presence, his physicality, that like a penetrating spotlight in a very dark alley, highlighted a parcel of knowledge, unspoken within Marj. By being there, in all his wobbling excess, Kevin gave Marj the authority to think big, to flirt with dangerous thoughts.

It had been a crisp morning. Watery early sun marked out the casuarinas as shadows on the ground. Molly's fingers ached as she pulled the cold wet washing out of a cane basket—she'd forgotten it from the day before. One by one she pegged the pieces in looping rows along the wire. A cloud of pigeons flew over the garden. Close to the ground and in a rush of wind and a flurry, it was the first flock she'd seen since arriving. Dozens of feathery wings vibrated and whistled overhead. They flew low, close enough for Molly to reach out and touch their black and white and bronze bodies. If she were to write to Joyce—and she'd tried many times with the thought too of sending a little money—she could talk about pigeons, and how she missed them. It would help she thought, for she wouldn't have to mention Jimmy, nor the fact that she was growing round with a child. It would be a cover for her real feeling.

The pigeons disappeared quickly.

Molly searched the blue expanse above her washing line for the speckled cloud of birds. She wanted them with her, to bomb her, whistle past in formation, and spiral closer to their destination with each swoop. She wanted them to stay afloat and drift with the wind, gliding backwards, to remind her of possibilities. For nostalgia's sake.

"He won't take no for an answer you know, so excitable," Marj was saying, coming to the fence, beckoning, her voice gliding on the crisp autumnal air, "And I've been cleaning, been giving the house a good airing, a thorough going over. It'll look nice for Barbara, for her shower party. You will be there won't you Molly, I've got to have you there, we could hand around food together and you'll get to meet all of Barb's friends, the bridesmaids. Don't know what's wrong with Kev though. Maybe the whole thing's getting to him."

Molly bit her lip. Her stomach heaved. It seemed the earth was turning faster than normal, giving her vertigo.

"I feel like dumping him in that hole of yours . . . so much is happening and I've got a lot on my mind! But it would be too small for his body. You should fill it in Molly, now that Jimmy's gone. It's a death trap as it is. It's a wonder he didn't do it before he left."

The air was cool with autumn on its way but Molly felt warm and flushed, then shivery, unsteady and dizzy all at the same time; wanting to hold her friend close, as she did in the car going to the Murrumbidgee, best of all return to the early days when Marj taught her everything, where ambition amounted to a line of sweet washing to fold indoors, eating roast lamb with gravy, and kissing loquat lips. But Marj was acting strangely, blocking the sun, maybe knowing something more, something indefensible, detached and loose, but also something demanding and accusing just as Molly's body knew with the dizziness, the bleeding, although the vomiting had ceased.

"You musn't leave the washing out too long in the afternoons now—the clothes become damp with this chill in the air. Remember that Molly, won't you and don't forget I want you there." With just a hint of bossiness, Marj was gone.

In hindsight, that's when the trouble began. Up until then Molly was proud of the way she'd been able to control things.

There was cohesion between the external world and a private interior. Silence was the great pacifier.

The dreams relating to that time are awash with the colour crimson and a great wobbling jelly. It sticks in Molly's throat and in the morning without fail there's a stench.

Two recurring images. One is of the colour crimson on her pants, a hint of things to come and just enough to raise the alarm in her mind. Despite meticulous washing, the stain never comes out. The other is of Kevin. For a time in a perplexing way she'd felt attached to him. She'd never have admitted it, although she knew it was to do with Marj. But in his presence, she was afraid.

bridal shower parties

FROM THE Waters' back door, Molly was able to scan everyone moulded in the warm yellow light before Marj could
feel her presence amidst the chatter. Spying again. She felt
hot, flushed. Molly put her hands to her throat.

The house was full of women, Barbara's friends, Barbara's bridesmaids, invited wedding guests bearing small gifts
for Barbara's new home—knives, egg whisks, washing
baskets, homemade peg bags, cake tins and sieves, and for the
more fashionable, coloured ceramic tea sets with matching
ramekins. The presents and their tissue wrappings and
ribbons would be piled high on the double bed. Molly's
hands were empty, Marj insisting she had done enough
already. The dresses and headpieces were complete, and
hung side by side from the picture rail in Molly's sewing
room. They would fit the bridal party without a tuck to
spare.

She saw Barbara too, there, in the door of the hallway,
leaning against the jamb and blocking the way to the rest
of the house. Barbara wasn't fat, so much as extra-large and
attractive. Her skin was smooth. Her hair was curly, long
and black like Marj's. And even from a distance Molly could
see that her eyes were milky blue like Kevin's. It was the contrast more than anything, the way those eyes let you enter
an eternal space, the facial features dissolving into a vortex.
Molly wondered why she hadn't met her before, for it was
Marj who arranged and oversaw the fittings. She would
have liked to have been a visible part of the family . . .

Molly closed her eyes. Just a little while ago, her sense of family had been complete, yet how quickly things can change in half a year, Jimmy leading the charge. Seduced, she'd sewn herself into the fabric of another family, with their child in her womb. She was close, perched now on the cusp of inclusion . . . yet . . . so far away. She ached inside with longing . . .

Molly had hoped to slip into the house, unnoticed. Marj would be there, somewhere, supervising the table, pouring drinks, and handing around tea plates and cake forks and selections of sweet food. Kevin would be home after everyone had left; he'd gone to the club for the evening. But before stepping a foot across the threshold into Marj's decorated and welcoming house, Molly felt a trickle. Deep inside the womb where mysterious things happen, the seed was letting go of its mooring.

What Molly remembers of that time, was being in the bath-room later, much later, after all the guests had gone, the house quite quiet. Marj found her there, on the floor in a corner, amongst the pink and white tiles, the glass knobs and bottles and jars. Curled in a ball, in a foetal position, Molly spoke with a relentless gibberish tongue amidst a growing pool of blood.

"I've lost my skin, my skin's fallen apart."

Thinking back, Molly wonders what it is that makes a child reject its parental body before it has a life of its own, before it can breathe alone, unsupported? Nature has you by the throat. You give birth to death and against your will a small part of yourself dies within.

It was Marj who cleaned up the mess. With bare hands she collected and wrapped everything she could into a clean linen tea-towel. She held the small bundle against her bosom, as she would her own child. It was a fleeting moment, but from out of the fog Molly caught a look of tenderness, feeling sure Marj must know more than she showed, but astonished too by her own jealousy, a smarting which clawed across her heart, holding it fast with pincers. Not only did Molly want to have her own child, Kevin's child if it had to be—to keep a link with Marj—but also, be that child, Marj's child, be held lovingly in her friend's arms.

Together, they paused in Molly's garden, cushioned by the darkness. Marj lifted the cloth bundle to her lips, kissed it, and threw it to the bottom of Jimmy's soil pit, while Molly buried it with armfuls of mottled clay. Not just then but later too, Molly grew to be madly jealous of the child buried in the Canberra garden, her child, and of the way Marj held and kissed the swaddling.

Back in Marj's house, Marj stripped off the bloodied clothes, washed Molly's body with a warm soapy cloth and dressed her in a clean nightdress. She laid her out on her bed between fresh sheets from off the line, smelling sweetly with caught sunlight. She patted her with a firm strong hand between the shoulder blades. Again and again. Pat, pat, pat. Working a definite rhythm on Molly's back. Conducting an orchestra with her right hand.

"Marj, can you sing . . . for me . . . please?" Molly asked in a whisper, her body still contracting.

"What?"

"Your song."

The words and notes drifted across the bed as if she were floating on water.

"Stop! Marj stop," Molly panted, struggling with her breath. "Okay, you can go on again, I'm sorry . . . go on."

She swam gently back to the surface. There was no fear of drowning amongst these supportive waves.

Where the ri-ver oh the sweet ri-ver flows Where the ri-ver the sweet sweet ri-ver flows Come home come home wash me clean Where the ri-ver oh the sweet ri-ver flows.

Sometime in the night Molly became aware of thick stubby toes and neatly cut nails lying next to her head in Marj's bed. Unsure of where she was, she awoke fully, hugging the feet closely to her chest between her breasts. They were distinctive feet with brown skin to the tips and hardened grey soles, and in the moonlight she saw they were cracked along the heel.

Marj's unmistakeable feet.

Marj's steady breathing.

If she tried hard she could remember the night before, the capable hands and soothing voice, the blood, her soaked clothes, and the beginnings of a baby in a tea-towel kissed and held by Marj. All the different parts of the story jumbled in her mind in a great whirl like a flummery mixture being whipped with a wooden spoon. And then there was Kevin, somewhere in the house in another room, passed out, drunk. It was no good thinking about his hands plastering her body. She *had* to be strong for Marj.

All in a rush but with nimble movements, she got out of the bed in order to turn around. She tucked herself in alongside Marj, so as to lie face to face. The smell of sleep encased them both and their loose hair intermingled. And quite spontaneously she kissed her. A loquat jelly kiss, a kiss to seal. With it she wanted to tell Marj how she loved her, how she loved Marj loving her, that she felt they were made of the same material, the one fruit.

Then, without pausing to think about what she was doing, nor about what Marj would say, Molly kissed Marj again on the lips, and then again and again, each time growing a little more bold. She craved Marj now, as never before. Coming in closer still, their breasts looped as one, she rubbed her pale skin against Marj's fat brown cheek. With gentle nibbles she took bites of Marj's lips as if she were tasting an exotic sweetmeat for the first time, intoxicated by its fleshy flavour. Marj all sleepy and with a murmur wrapped her ample arms around Molly's smaller frame and to Molly's surprise didn't reprimand her for her foolishness but gave in to it too, drawing Molly's face and body into her own, shutting out the marauding, unanswered questions, the sadness.

Like the world outside encased in deep darkness, hours before the first sense of light, the two lay together in an envelope of their own beneath the covers. Molly and Marj were feasting.

The pain cradled by her pelvis had subsided now to an irregular flutter. Her thighs were more numb than laced with cramps, no longer restless and fighting against the thickening and shortening of the uterine muscle. She was still, not wanting to break the pose; calm, with the taste of something new on her lips. She kept guard as the other slept. She didn't dare move for fear of waking her friend, for fear of that moment, that embrace, ending. Wedged into the bed, her body made a well-defined warm patch between the sheets, and against Marj.

In the morning, drawn together by the turn of events, but never mentioning the details of that excursion once awake, they held each other while perched on the side of the bed. It had been a snatched moment of comfort, unsustainable in the harsh morning light. If Molly blinked, it would go.

Marj said, "You've got to look things straight in the eye Molly."

They ate a breakfast of hot buttered toast in long fingers. Droplets of steam warmed the blue-rimmed china plates in their hands. And the dust caught in the morning light shone as dazzling specks of glitter.

Marj said, "You can't be afraid of things you don't know about, things you don't see."

Molly's lips were dry and cracked. She kept silent about the dull thudding pain, and that stab of knowing and of being known. That private joy!

"I'll take you to the hospital Molly, you'll need to be checked."

Alone the next night, she dreamt of bodies. Fragments stuck together, overlapping. Molly woke in a sweat. The sky peeled above her in strips of grey rain.

pupal skins

NOBODY KNOWS what triggers the most remarkable change in an insect's life. The shape of an adult insect is moulded within the confines of a silky pupal skin, in private, secretly. The eating and gorging on the carcass is finished. The motionless pupa only breathes.

Pupa means doll.

It is a change of heart, of direction.

a warm body suit

IN THE early morning of Easter Saturday, Barbara's wedding day, Molly delivered the consignment of dresses to Marj's house. She let herself in through the kitchen, pausing only to listen to sleepy heavy breathing and to hang up the load, safely. Her arms were crowded with white and cream lace, clouds of beaded tulle clumped together around a coronet, green and yellow silk, a small apricot dress with a purple ribbon, white feathery curvettes for the bridesmaids' heads hanging from her wrists, and an olive green ensemble for the bride's mother. She wore Marj's hat on her head, its wide brim covered with real flowers.

Before having breakfast, Molly went for a walk in the bush behind their two houses. She climbed through the hole in the fence, jagged in places, and scrambled up the rocky ridge. She was conscious only of a growing desire, a necessity, to see a broad sweep of the town and her mountains.

She breathed in gasps, shallow, painful. Her head pounded from deep inside, in a groove down the right temple. Thud. Thud. She was still bleeding. Thud. Thud. With each heavy step.

. . . to rise above the sleepiness, stand over the houses, Marj's house, try and find it in the mist . . .

Her body worked hard.

. . . one foot in front of the other, lift the thigh, hand on the knee for support, up, up, up, it was never this high, this steep . . .

She climbed Mount Ainslie to witness a view of morning

on her mountains, the bush women in their steamy bath. She wanted to bathe there too amidst the limp gossamer. To feel the warm steam seep through her skin. To cover herself with a timeless cloak that belonged, a robe her size.

. . . a warm body suit, no gusset, no seam, no tucks ...

Her work was complete. The day had arrived at last.

. . . all that fuss for a few hours, who was she marrying?— a shadow, but work does pay . . . Marj has paid in full before it's finished, my sandalwood suit looks nice, shapely . . . seize something new and fresh . . .

Marj said she would take her to Holy Communion on Sunday for the Easter morning service, after all the fuss of the wedding had ceased. They'd enjoy the carefully chosen flowers and ribbons in peace, and witness a resurrection together. They would taste the bread and wine in unison, as joint partners to the body of Christ.

Sweat trickled. Early morning dew hung suspended from the eucalypt leaves. The drops waited, trembling, for the full weight of pearly water to congregate, for the completion of their shape, before letting go.

. . . I can sew, I can cook now, I know how to wash, I can hang out the clothes under any sky, I can eat bread and drink wine . . . I know when to put it in my mouth . . . those things of the body . . . Marj talks about doing exceptional things . . .

"I'll show you fruit that counts," Molly could hear Marj say. "We'll go up north, Molly, to the mango country and eat the flesh down to its hairy seed. Feel squashed yellowy-green buttery avocado pears under our feet, between our toes, oozing out, as cold as smooth saturated mud. I'll show you how to cut a pawpaw, peel back the bitter blotchy skin, spoon out the black rubbery slippery seeds and eat the orange fruit tossed and coated in sugar, for dessert."

I'm full already . . . the feasting is over . . .

"We'll eat together, on our verandah up north."

. . . Marj dreams, she dreams of past things, of impossible things, she dreams only dreams . . .

From the top, Molly took in a full autumnal view of the valley, and the Brindabellas beyond. She stood astride ancient rock overlooking the intersecting avenues of pink and red and yellow leaves peeking through an eggwhite mist.

. . . I'll come back and visit, I'll see you all again . . . when the lake fills up . . . when the heart is found . . .

Alone, vulnerable. But up high with a view.

Down the hill in the throbbing weight of silence between the walls of her house, Molly packed a small cardboard box, her sewing machine, a hatbox, her fingers heavy with the work. Into her pyjama bag she emptied bottles of brown and silver coins which stood in a perfect rectangular grid system on Jimmy's windowsill behind the drawn blind. She knotted the opening with a long black shoelace. She could always come back, she comforted herself with the thought.

Lastly, she scribbled a note and pinned it down on the kitchen table with the dish of Queensland nuts and the twin bottles of water:

> *Had to go Marj, leave you to Barbara.*
> *I'm going to see if what you say is*
> *true about up north.*
> *Molly xxx*

Slipping out the door, she was on her way.

But it didn't end there. For with no preconceived thought and simply because the idea presented itself, there, hanging on Marj's line in amongst a host of other last-minute washing, Molly did something she'd never dream of doing before this. As if under sedation and with an incantation of words ringing in her ears—*flatten them, shake them, crack and flick them, otherwise they stick for the sun's a blessing and a curse*—she stole one of Marj's dresses. It was quite spontaneous and she had no regrets. She stole the one without sleeves with a gathered circular neckline, the one that had swirled over Marj's fatness the day they got wet.

That dress was to become a lifeline, a source of inspiration for all those years of waiting. In a way, even though it brought Marj oh so close whenever she dressed up in it, in private, at times when she was alone, swirling through the rooms of her many houses and flats, that dress with its green and blue bouquets, also, somehow, pushed a wedge between her and her loved one. By possessing one of Marj's dresses in that animistic way, indeed by supplanting her own body into that of Marj's, Molly had suspended the need to see her in person.

Underneath the Hill's hoist in Marj's garden, the dress just dropped into Molly's waiting hands, like a piece of ripe fruit. With it tucked under her arm, she simply walked away.

PART THREE

an Easter moon

LIE LOW *Molly dear, lie low and wait.* That's what she can hear Marj advising across the years and years of waiting. It is a faint calling now, a whispering willy-willy of sound, a pulse.

Remember Marj?

Remember the bush, that first home?

How can Molly forget the dry smell of a Canberra summer caught in the folds of a cotton dress, or the lazy purple mountains lying against an expanse of blue? How can she forget the trill of laughter cascading through the whirr of an egg-beater and then seeing her fingers, curled tightly, bone-white on the undersides of oven-baked brown? Remember Marj, how can she forget, licking and kissing, the sweet loquat lips over buttery early morning toast?

Just below the surface these memories of infatuation lie in wait. They feed off the fat of the land. They multiply rapidly in the tropical fruit bowl of Queensland. They wait for confirmation and release.

She'd say, *If you wait long enough, you'll get fed in the end, for there's always a feast.* But wait for what? For somebody to take the lead, to show her the way? In the roll of time Molly has drifted, so that a circular dreaming has seized her. She twirls within the folds of a stolen garment, linking arms with the absent friend. In her dreams day and night, Molly performs the dance of the mandala.

Then one day, caught up in a dance of his own, Jimmy wrote a letter. Out of the blue, it is enough to break the spell. The day after it arrived, Molly found herself storming along Mudjimba Beach.

She knew the beach was a necessary backdrop for the start of something, along that changeable zip between solid land and watery depths. On sand it is possible to experiment, to sculpture a thought, while remaining aware of the erosion, attuned to the ebbing of the tides. In spite of its vulnerability, it feels safe. Along the coastline north of Maroochydore, a little less urbanized, protected by reserves and national parks, this coastline beginning at Mudjimba is a jewel, a sparkling contrast to the coastal plain stretching south. Down there, the money-makers flex their developmental muscle while remaining unconcerned about the delicate nature of the ground they churn with steel and concrete claws.

Molly looks out across the flat grey-green colour of the Coral Sea, to Mudjimba Island, the Old Woman, a hump rising from off the deep seabed.

Lie low and wait.

Oh God yes, the two words *lie low* burrow in under the skin. She'd kept the words as a text for life, reciting them over and over, managing the act to perfection, they became the habit. But Molly knows it is over. The waiting is done and she now has to act.

Sydney and miles of open bush and farmland and a flat and empty Lake George lie behind them as they cruise along a dual highway in the chocolate-coloured Chrysler. The girls are awake but refuse even the suggestion of breakfast, their stomachs queasy and full of fruit from the binge the night before.

"Well, Kate, Sarah, welcome to Canberra. This is it!" Molly's hearty voice masks the trepidation she feels.

A spread of green suburbs, too many to count and hidden amongst forests of trees, swirl in an artificial basket around the foot of Black Mountain and beyond, surging south, up and over small hills, towards Tharwa and Cooma and the high country.

"How do you know Canberra Mum?" Kate asks.

"I've been here before."

"So who's this Marj person you're so keen to see?" Sarah's question this time.

"A friend . . . from the past, my past."

"You mean you didn't come straight to Brisbane?" She looks at Molly quizzically.

"No. Canberra."

"Okay Mum, so what's the big deal?" Kate wants to know.

"I like the way she cooks."

"So?"

"She loves food."

"You mean she's fat?"

"Yeah, you could say she's fat."

"God I hate fat people. They make me sick." Kate is on a fruit diet, of sorts.

"That's unfair Kate. Mum it's okay, we'll fit in." Sarah touched Molly on the shoulder, for support.

After booking into the caravan park, Molly makes straight for Ainslie. Now, so close to her destination, she pushes forward, aware there's no room for hesitation or escape. She drives as if she's slightly intoxicated, incautious but alert.

On the threshold to Marj's house she says to the person opening the door, without hesitation, "Barbara, it's me, Molly, do you remember?" At the door, Barbara towers over Molly in an extra-large off-white tee-shirt with shoulder pads. Molly discovers she's easy to recognize with her familiar moon face. She's a fake blonde now, hair straight and long and split, shoulder length, with a snake of grey for a parting pulled back over a widow's peak, a row of black and rusted bobby pins either side. Pockets of shadows hang in sacs around her button blue eyes poised high on cheeks smudged with enough rouge to match the gloss on the lips. Yet despite her looks, indeed because of them, Molly can't help but notice a similarity with her mother. Molly wants Barb to shout her name, to show some enthusiasm. Instead, Barbara says with restraint: "Mum's in hospital did you know?"

"Hospital?"

"Cataracts. Complications. Doesn't know how to look after herself. She's in the Royal Canberra, down by the lake. The op's on Monday. You knew that I suppose, you two were such good friends."

Molly wobbles on her legs a little. But Barbara has charm and to her surprise Molly finds she wants to please. "I didn't know she was in hospital." She doesn't confess to them not keeping in touch at all.

Barbara says, "I'm glad she's there. It gives me a break. A very difficult patient for them, they all try to please her too much I think. She's nuts just like she always was, nothing changes."

Standing on the threshold of Marj's house, Molly feels comforted. She finds talking with her daughter one of the most natural things in the world. It is as if everyone welcomes unexpected people from out of the past into their lives as friends. Molly can't wait to see Marj for herself.

Little else attracts her, just then, her old house with the flypaper (it looks smaller anyway, too ordered, and nothing compared to the airy graciousness of the weatherboard houses on stilts she'd grown used to), the yards at the back with the Hills hoists, the burial ground and pink stone birdbath . . .

All she needs to see is her friend.

Marj.

Before anything else.

The rest doesn't matter for the moment.

She leaves some pawpaws with button-eyed Barb.

"I've lost my appetite." A voice speaks from across the public ward. A three-garden voice.

"You'll soon be able to eat, now we'll just get you up in the bed, there's the girl. Up a bit more."

"Barb's in my house of course."

"Yes Mrs Waters. Don't worry about it, everything will be all right."

"I bet the washing is still in the basket." The voice is agitated.

"Mrs Waters, I do understand, right now there's someone to see you."

"Wet and smelly."

"Now, you want to look nice for your visitor, don't you, she's brought you something. You're a lucky one."

"Mouldy grey in the creases."

"Of course, you're concerned about it, but now you've got a visitor to think of, Molly Moone she said her name was, and she's come all the way from Queensland, Maroochydore I think she said."

"She's lazy, good-for-nothing, married a rich man to slob around and eat. She'll eat herself to the grave and it's all takeaways. At least I cooked. She's a lazy dog. Couldn't hang out that damned washing to save herself." The patient's voice booms. Her words slip out with ease, she's been talking for a lifetime. "I don't see her, even though we live in the same house. Feels like I'm boarding. Molly . . . did you say Molly? Molly *Rose?*"

"Molly Moone. She says you know her and she's come to visit you."

A breeze tunnels through an open window into the surgical ward and the loose hospital screen billows around the bed, in waves.

The visitor watches the shadow puppetries from across the ward, her eyes and ears alert, catching every detail. Her hair is bleached by the sun and wrapped in a scarf secured with a pin. She wears flat shoes and a spotted shapely dress over her freckled skin. In one hand, she clutches a black purse, a brown paper bag and flowers, and in the other, a fat lemon. She knows who lies on the starched sheets behind the curtain: the voice is old, but unmistakeable. The fruit in her hand seems to grow in size. A hard swollen ball. An Easter moon. Pressing into her palm.

It is such a shock.

Molly now stands on the inside of the curtain walls.

Her Marj.

The nurse is saying, "Easy does it Mrs Waters, remember you've got a drip, let go of your visitor now, there's the girl, easy."

Her friend.

"Are you all right then?"

Her body.

Marj.

It is such a shock, her *body*, a shell of a body, a dried out and shrivelled-in-the-sun body, a skin-and-bone body, just as though her fat like breath itself had been sucked from around her bones, leaving a balloon of thin transparent skin. A pupal skin. An empty cocoon. Had the imago flown?

"I've been expecting you." The body speaks, metamorphosis. *I've been expecting you.*

Her voice.

The words fall like soft rain into silence, clear and unmistakeable, but somehow reassuring enough to make Molly grow warm at the thought of Marj's mind being filled all those years with the possibilities of meeting again.

Marj continues, "I thought I'd lost you Molly. I thought I'd lost you forever." Her arms are thin and transparent and pearl-blue: she was *fat* once. Muscles flap around the bone, as loosely as the wrinkled flesh of a dried fig. They were taut, brown, hardened, skin stretched, good-looking before.

But she still has strength to hold!

And she wears *that* dress, how can that be? Refusing the starched whiteness of the backless ones worn in hospital, Marj is covered in crimplene flowers cut on the bias with flared capped sleeves. An oversized bow of loops and tags at her breast hides the now-absent cleavage and soft cushion fullness. The dress she wears must be a twin to the stolen one.

"Can I leave you to it?" The nurse wants to know.

"I'm an old friend. I'll be right." Molly reassures, fearing her own hesitation.

"I knew you would come back."

Molly wanted to get past the flowers and bows and into her neighbour's skin, a long time ago.

"Yes, we'll be right, won't we Marj?" Molly says, her own voice consoling herself.

She wanted to imitate Marj, once.

islands of affection

OUTSIDE THE hospital neat parcels of suburbs and monuments and gardens, north and south, lie collected around Lake Burley Griffin with its weeping willows and reeds, the watery heart throbbing. The majestic Brindabellas guard the city with fleshy round curves. A mower hums and the lemon-smell of scented grass clippings wafts through the open window.

"It was time to come to Canberra and see you," the visitor volunteers as a beginning. She sits perched on the edge of the bed.

The patient shakes, her fig-flesh wobbly and loose.

"Before I die!"

"Marj . . ." Her old friend is uncanny despite everything, breathing on her with force. She disarms Molly, making it safe to relax. She soothes her as touching the silk lining of a pocket would. Marj unmasks her by fostering a physical intimacy as easily as eating jam and warm buttery toast together with the ceiling fans whirring.

To subdue her excitement, Molly passes the lemon she's been holding. She passes it reverently, like a wafer for communion. A yellow Easter moon. Perfection, she decides, is a matter of timing, of knowing when to give the fruit. "Anything grows up there, you were right," she says.

Some plans do work out.

"Mouldy grey on their bottoms." Marj says, her voice is flat. "She wouldn't know what to do with one and I bet they're rotting on the ground. Didn't I find a dead lemon under the dresser? Shrivelled and dried out, its juice gone? My eyes are a mess now, they've decided. I can't see you with these cataracts—that's what they're going to try and fix up —just another body to dress for the grave."

In a large coffee bottle, Molly stands up the tired pink carnations she's brought. Flowers are essential, Marj always grew and gave the best.

"I'm not an invalid," Marj continues, ignoring the flower arrangement at first, "I feel like a prisoner here, but you are a dear to bring me something. I'd love to get to Queensland, all those mangoes and avocados. I just breathe the word and I can taste them in my mouth. We used to feed them to the dogs you know . . ." She fondles the lemon.

"The kids couldn't come," Molly says, wanting to place herself in some sort of context, yet unsure of how to break the spell Marj has a hold of.

". . . Did you know the avocado has bisexual parts? We'd stomp on them with bare feet, sliding with the slippery stone, our soles spread with green butter. Mum'd go mad, she hated the stains on the carpet. A hell of a job cleaning them up too. A hose was good, her spraying, us screaming . . ."

"I've left them in the car Marj, parked under a shady tree overlooking the muddy water, with ice blocks melting down their arms probably." Molly interrupts again, filling the conversation with relevant detail, the gaping hole in the ground and its four walls with shovelfuls of mottled clays. It feels like a weak form of show-and-tell but Marj doesn't seem to sense her there. Was that hole of Jimmy's ever filled in?

". . . They loved them. Green mouths. Good first solids. In my day that is, I've lost count, but you couldn't get them in this sweet place. Too far south. Not the real Australia . . ."

"Their names are Kate and Sarah."

"How many?" Ah, at last it seems Marj is willing to make a connection.

"Twins."

"How many lemons have you grown? You couldn't do anything without me. You were helpless then, both cowering in the corner like scared white mice, afraid I was going to chop off your heads!!" Her laugh rattles. "Ah Jimmy, he was sandy, ran through your fingers, pink tongue hanging. Whatever happened to Jimmy?" Marj turns to face Molly. It's with that look, Molly's thinking. It's the same look that she'd treasured in her mind, dim though it was if she'd been forced to describe it, but now so obvious. Molly winces with recogniton. Hard to believe she is experiencing it first hand. A penetrating look. A look of feasting. One demanding reciprocity. God it feels good, she thinks.

Molly says, "He cut me loose, gave me my own head." Now that it's there, she wants to build on the silky thread spun between them.

"Where's he now?" Marj asks. At last they are conversing with some sort of order, weaving a delicate web.

"Funny you should say that," Molly thinks of him and the letter he'd written, with affection . . . *I thought we could just see each other again.* If only Marj knew the reason for her coming to Canberra, his catalytic move, then she'd have to thank Jimmy for something.

"Go on," Marj encourages her.

"Well," Molly begins carefully, "he's coming out to visit. Soon."

"Oh . . ." Marj seems disappointed. "He wasn't built for this place you know."

Molly follows on quickly, "He won't stay. Just a visit. It excites me. He'll never try migrating again I'm sure." She talks fast to fit in, trying to establish some confidence within herself as well as within her old friend. She empties the brown paper bag she has brought into the bedside locker, keen to finish her work. To return north a new person. To partake in a communion with her friend. Licorice Allsorts, Minties, Milk Bottles and Bullets spill out into the drawer, all in two-dollar plastic bags she'd grabbed from a 24-hour all-service petrol-stop-and-shop. She shuts the drawer with a bang, aware of a dull throbbing pain in her chest.

"Everyone's a migrant here Molly, except the originals I suppose. How many bags of lollies have you given me you angel? You have to forgive because you love. I taught you that."

"Four, I can bring more if you like," Molly says.

"I'll get fat! Anyway, I can't eat, I go under on Monday. The nurse looks in there every day."

"Just tell her not to."

"Him."

"Him then."

"Queensland," Marj interrupts, unsettling her visitor. "Left my run too late. I don't have to pretend any longer. I just breathe the word and I can taste them in my mouth . . ."

The ward clatters around them with trolleys and cups of tea, bedpans and cleaning mops and distant voices. Ignoring the cacophony, the two women sit on the bed behind pulled curtains, engrossed in their own worlds.

". . . We'd stomp on them with bare feet, sliding with the slippery stone, our soles spread with green butter . . ." Marj's eyes water, staring, trying to focus. She mops them with a large handkerchief.

There's a palpable pause. Like an organic being, it sits between the two women. Molly feels sure she can touch it, squeeze it, wrap her arms around it, move it to one side. But she doesn't. That pulse of silence has its place. Her mind wanders. She wonders if there will be enough time to climb Mount Ainslie. Or could she possibly get up Tidbinbilla, the one in the centre of her picture. Be part of the life crawling over the fleshy sides. But her chest is tight, there's a dull throb just below the surface.

"Twins hey?" Marj asks, breaking up whatever it is between them with her voice.

"Yeah."

"I like the names. If I had more girls, I would have given

them names like that—Kate, Sarah, Sarah, Kate . . . I never thought you could do it." Again, Marj looks at Molly as she speaks. This time it's a look laced with admiration, Molly feels sure.

She senses a shift of affection.

Can it be that her children, born out of unhappiness because of her need of love, bring her close, at last?

As if in reply Molly pushes through the invisible barrier. She pushes through that pulse which before had been so forcible in separating them out. Her hands crawl along the white sheets. She never thought it would be this hard. They clasp and claw and crawl until, with great determination, the two friends hug and hug for a very long time, a reminder of that pleasure in the past. Together they form an island surrounded by choppy water, their silence encased by the chatter and commotion of a busy surgical ward.

the missing pearl

IT IS only by being in Marj's presence again that Molly begins to see things for what they are, things that up until then were shrouded in layers of silk, built up over time by the slippery, even sly, nature of memory. At first she doesn't want to believe, for the protected state of being hidden in a cocoon is altogether comfortable, warm and safe. If she is to leave that place, she is afraid she'll be overwhelmed again, snapped up, swallowed by a greater, larger body than her own, lost and not found. But with a good view of Marj, Molly senses it is time to be courageous.

On Easter morning Molly visits Marj early and stays by her side till lunch is served and on through the patients' rest in the afternoon. Women in starched uniforms, with plates of warm sliced meat and peppery white sauce, smile indifferently as they drift past Mrs Marjory Waters and her drip and the sign above her bed—*nil by mouth*.

Molly holds her friend's hand and waits for an angel, any angel, to roll back the heavy stone. She doesn't care how long it takes.

It is Marj who comes to the point early. "You never came to church with me," she says.

"You remember?" Molly asks.

"It was a terrible day. How could I forget? Barbara lied and told everyone she'd made the dresses in her spare time. At the reception she blamed me for everything, the stuff-ups."

"Why did Barbara blame you?" Molly thinks back to how charming Barbara had been to her on the front doorstep.

219

Marj laughs with a wheeze, mouth open in a slit without teeth. Ignoring the question as if the answer was self-evident, she says, "She's been up here once, very expensive flowers, damn the money, damn her, but the flowers are always the best. You've fattened a little, just look at me!" Marj flaps the handkerchief around her arms.

"And Kevin . . . what about Kev?"

"Oh Kev wasn't any help, he just got drunk. Since he's gone, I've lived out the back of the house, her house now she says, but I've kept my garden."

"When did he . . ."

"He died a few years later. Heart. The drink killed him."

Molly winces and fingers the mustard curtain surrounding the bed. Her eyes narrow. She knows she has to get closer to the heart of things before she leaves, to come clean. *Try spreading the jam with a knife.* "Jimmy didn't know anything about it Marj, about the baby . . ."

"Yeah I know, you didn't tell him."

"No Marj, I mean . . . he didn't know anything about it . . . before . . ."

Marj snorts and says, "Surely he must, a man *knows* Molly."

"Marj . . . Jimmy didn't know, because he couldn't . . ." She falters, she can't say it, "he c–couldn't." Her skin prickles with heat as she feels his body withdraw and curl into itself. "It wasn't J–J– . . ."

The knife is sharp. Molly is afraid she'll cut herself. How much easier it would be if Jimmy were dead, she thinks. This thought had resurfaced from time to time. With it she hoped to cure the itching sore once and for all. But she knows the dead linger on. Like Joyce Moone, Jimmy had lodged himself into her story. He would remain a shadowy presence, perhaps a treacherous one if the light were to fall his way just now: *Rosy, Rosy,* a shrill call reverberates from across the other side of the world, *I want you.* To her surprise, it is a call that sets Molly trembling with a shudder. And even after the commotion has subsided, there's a throb where the waves once were.

On the bed beside her, Marj is silent, the blue skin gives nothing away. Marj must have smelt the difference back then, surely. Molly did. She must have cradled the knowledge in her ample arms when the younger woman aborted. Anyone could see Jimmy couldn't . . .

In rehearsal, Molly knew some things about meeting again would be straightforward, automatic. Hugging Marj to lean against the clipped kiss-curls bordering her face. Yes. She knew she would touch Marj's skin again, lick her paperwhite lips in a kiss, smell her oil, hear her voice, remember being together, maybe laugh and cry and . . .

But . . .

Molly waits for a response.

Does Marj remember how to talk, how to *really* talk, to her? Does she know what happened back then? The nasty possibility of complicity continues to lurk in Molly's mind.

Then Marj says, "Molly . . ." Her bones seem to collapse as she speaks. "I . . . knew." Two words. She knew. What, exactly?

"What? About Jimmy?" Oh yes, how simple it is to see into other people's lives, Molly is thinking.

The eyes of the old woman roll to white. She's in her late seventies now. Is Molly being too harsh? Faded lashes wash the blue and capillary-red blotchy cheek. The hands shake, then the head wobbles, as she leans back on the pillows for support. Molly watches Marj's mouth, for there, at last, the words come out, deliberately, as she once ate food, rolling her wet tongue around the syllables, in luxury. "It could only have happened in one way," Marj says with just a little insistence. "I knew him, I knew him. I knew Kev well." Marj's voice isn't accusing, but tired, resigned to sharing a secret. There is a long pause. "I found them *both* . . . a lemon . . . and . . . an earring . . . *your* earring . . . It fell down between the beds. Your pearl earring. It was then that I knew for sure what I'd known in my heart all along."

Molly is thinking, shouting, caught in the folds of inter-secting story-lines. She puts her hands up to her ears, to feel the place of the missing pearls. He did it Marj, she wants to say, don't blame yourself. From the Garden of Eden Adam says thanks very much, I like fruit: I even like sugar-coated frosted rose petals if it comes to that. She can't look Marj in the eye. As a caution, she stares out onto the flat opaque surface of the lake.

Now, the curtained room feels small and still, without fresh air. The rings on the rail creak. People die in these wards, she's thinking. Her mother died in one. They pass out with smothered screams, begging for a final handclasp, the bedclothes ruffled in the struggle, into the unknown, alone. Washed bodies are covered with white sheets. Nurses run. Thin metal tubes rattle like food trolleys. Cleaners douse all that remains in Dettol. Splash and air out the death beds.

Before Marj told her—she'd said, *I knew*—the possibility of her knowing was merely a thought, a drifting, toxic reed in the turbulent water. If she swam hard, Molly escaped its poison. Whereas now with this revelation, Molly feels trapped, anchored to the seabed by the very small claws along the reed's edging. And yet, there, from out of the tumult with the claws pinching her skin, she hears a voice, familiar music . . .

Still leaning back against the cushion of pillows, Marj is saying in such a gentle way, "Did you think I'd let you down love? You know I wouldn't do that. I didn't tell you because there was no need. You didn't need to know that then. I didn't have the heart. Besides, I needed you as you were then. To feast with me. There wasn't room for anyone or anything else." Marj sings the words with all the liquid grace Molly remembers her for.

The younger woman listens with shame, with a creeping sense of guilt that she'd ever doubted Marj, even blamed her for her husband's action.

And yet, there is something missing, but she can't put her finger on it. The pain she had to cradle seems to have been ignored. A diluted anger boils over. He ate your glorious food, she wants to shout, then swam his fat, that carnival of excess, above my body making me drown while black flies danced in pairs above the bed. Rape of any kind is unforgiveable. And if you knew . . . then why didn't you say something? . . . do something? . . . She wants to say you have to listen to my story for a change Marj. She tries to concentrate on a reply, but opens and shuts her mouth without a sound.

Marj continues: "I knew Jimmy couldn't raise his finger to save himself, let alone his dick to have a child. Don't blush Molly dear, it's just the truth."

Ah the truth, Molly thinks. Is that the ingredient that went missing? But where and how far do truths overlap?

"Now Kev on the other hand," Marj swims through her chosen words with such assurance. "Now there's a wanderer . . ." But she pauses. She too, as Molly had been, is caught. Molly waits with her, watching, listening, hardly daring to breathe. Isn't it this, above all else, that married people fear? Criticism of a partner, and so an implicit criticism of themselves? Molly remembers Kevin Waters in all his wobbling excess, looming large, and Marj's fingers curled around his at the tea table. She'd thought at the time that Marj tamed Kev. Perhaps the truth was mixed, contradictory, that Marj's action somehow disciplined an aberrant part of her own self, brought their collective house to order.

Marj continues, "I don't blame him Molly, it's gone. In the past isn't it? Blame doesn't help things. Let it be." She hesitates a little, then says, laying her hand over Molly's, "Molly dear if you want to know . . . it was too awful a thought, so I didn't think it at the time, I couldn't. I think I was a bit jealous of you. Does that make me gutless? Not to have said anything? We all had to survive didn't we?"

As Marj talks, feelings of anger and resentment and confusion peel away like the soft orange skin from around a ripe mandarin. Marj's words baptise her as her song did years ago, *Where the river oh the sweet river flows*.

"At least I knew you and I loved you and I could take great care of you and I did. I couldn't let you down," Marj speaks with confidence now. "Remember the outing to the river and the way I sang to you after you miscarried. We needed each other then. I found your earring and I've kept it as a memento."

"Ah the earring," Molly murmurs. She had been silent for so long, listening. Her voice trails, "Jimmy gave me those earrings on our engagement. They matched the string my mother gave me, with the gold safety catch," she pauses, to continue after a little time, "I knew I lost one . . . I thought you might find it . . ." Her hands begin to tingle. It feels strange to be talking now, as if in a different language. As she speaks of complexities, crashing waves wash across her face. But she's not afraid. They spill over an imaginary waterfall and down onto the lower stave, pushing the green water high into the sky in a white spray. It's hard to keep the heart in line and at one with the head. Molly wants the waves to roll ashore and lose speed. In the shallows up the face of wet sand, they'd fold back on themselves like a rolled hem of a lace dress.

"In my cabinet, Molly," Marj is saying, "I keep it with me always, in my old blue vinyl beauty case, tucked into the compartment in the middle, under the mirror. It's in the circular tin with MR on its bottom, that's right, the rose tin. Used to be a powder puff for my cheeks when I wore make-up in the early years when I thought that sort of thing mattered."

(And what happened to the other lone earring, the one in a nest of its own? After she had failed to pawn it years before on arrival in Brisbane, it disappeared into the dress-ups box, later rescued by Sarah and worn on her first date.)

Molly picks out a single screw-on pearl earring. She replaces the powder puff tin with a rose on its lid back into the blue vinyl beauty case, and gazes at the telltale trophy. Fingers uncoil. Marj, frail old Marj, holds the other side of the case. *Did you think I'd let you down love? You know I wouldn't do that. You knew I loved you.* Mudjimba Island, the old woman, lies low off the Sunshine Coast in the Coral Sea. The island, the centre of all, the mother, indissoluble, life-force, woman.

Molly holds the pearl in the cup of her hand. The pearl shines against the pink sea of Molly's skin. *Besides, I needed you. To feast with me. There wasn't room for anyone else.* This pearl in her hand, this island, this heart.

take and eat

THE WARD'S lunch has come and gone. The moment of departure is nearing: for all her travelling, the journey is only at the beginning. The quiet of a siesta stretches on into the distance. There's an eternal quality about the place.

Marj pulls open the locker drawer and passes an unwrapped Mintie to Molly.

"Here, we were always good at doing this, feasting together, but don't tell anyone will you Molly dear, they'll never forgive me if they have to use a stomach pump tomorrow morning before my op." She laughs easily now.

You chew on it this is my body.

Marj concludes the ritual, as if they are kneeling on a tapestry cushion taking communion, by passing a glass of cold water between them, tinkling with ice cubes. She says, "I am a bit dry."

Drink up it's my blood.

"I didn't think you believed all of that, really." Molly says.

"Sometimes it's useful," her old friend admits with a rueful smile, "Like now." The Mintie wrap flutters to the polished floor.

a lesson in flying

A PATH curls up around the base where the trees are thick and tall, and the smell sweetly moist. But to get to the top, you must leave the path eventually, push through a spread of bracken and rocky outcrops along a ridge and climb up and up and up to the place where the mountain humps, once viewed from the other side of the limestone plain and the Murrumbidgee valley, lie pressed against an expanse of blue, blue, blue skin.

They push and puff their way skywards, a hand resting on a knee for support as they clamber over the boulders, step by step, the other hand at every chance grasping the smooth and slender form of the snow gums and of the smaller branches of the peppermints. Heads are bowed for easy breathing and sweat trickles over their eager but tired bodies. Flanked either side by her daughters, Molly is amongst those lounging curves, amongst friends, the undefiled bush women.

Close to the top, Sarah asks, "Will you tell us now Mum? Who is this Marj person? I still don't understand."

Pausing for breath, Molly feels the question and a million suitable answers reverberate back and forth across the valley in a whirlpool of broken sentences and loose words, making the air thick with meaning. And she sees Marj for the last time at the hospital window appearing like a saint in a lunette, pressed up against the glass and waving, dim though it was because of the position of the setting sun.

"Yes I will Sarah," her voice falters a little, as if practising her new language, "I'll tell you."

"I'd like to know about it too," Kate pipes in, "And where your friend Jimmy fits in, it all sounds really juicy."

Molly laughs. "It was, Kate, believe me," she says. And with a note of certainty in her voice that she would never have thought possible at the beginning of the week, she tells them both, "We'll go home this afternoon. It's a long drive back to Queensland, but I'll tell you the whole story on the way."

"Everything?" they both ask in unison.

"Everything."

imago **1.** the final and fully developed stage of an insect after all metamorphoses, e.g. a butterfly or beetle. **2.** *Psychoanal.* an idealised concept of a loved one, formed in childhood and retained uncorrected in adult life.

Sweet River

Words: Francesca Rendle-Short   Music: Glyn Lehmann

Where the ri - ver oh the sweet river flows Where the ri - ver the sweet sweet ri - ver flows _____ Come home come home wash _____ me clean _____ Where the ri - ver oh the sweet _____ ri - ver flows.